MYRA DUFFY

WHEN OLD GHOSTS MEET

First Published in 2009 by YouWriteOn.com

Copyright © Text Myra Duffy

This revised edition 2013 published by FeedaRead

British Library C.I.P.

A CIP catalogue record for this title is available from the British Library

MYRA DUFFY

WHEN OLD GHOSTS MEET

The first Alison Cameron Mystery

(New Edition)

www.myraduffy.co.uk

http://myraduffy-awriterslot.blogspot.com

Twitter: @duffy_myra

Cover design by Mandy Sinclair

Also by Myra Duffy

The Isle of Bute series

The House at Ettrick Bay

Last Ferry to Bute

Last Dance at the Rothesay Pavilion

To Peter

With thanks for his many years of support

GHOST: Soul of dead person appearing to living; apparition; spectre.

(Oxford English Dictionary)

PROLOGUE

Two days before my birthday, I saw a ghost.

In my rush to catch the train, I decided to take the short cut from the High Street down to the back entrance at Waverley Station. I held on tightly to the iron handrails for support, hampered by my very smart, but very uncomfortable, new boots.

My only thought was to head for home and relax in front of the fire with a glass of wine. With a bit of luck, I'd be in time for the early train to Glasgow and be snug and warm by five o'clock. It was the end of a long hard week and the meeting I'd left - a whole day in the Cowgate Hotel, wrestling with colleagues over so-called innovative teaching methods - hadn't helped.

As soon as was decent, I gathered up my papers and said goodbye, pretending not to hear the 'Going to the station, Alison?' on my way to catch the lift down to the foyer.

A few minutes later and I was out into the fierce Edinburgh wind that takes your breath away, running across Market Street and over the pedestrian crossing as the lights went to amber.

I slowed my pace to pick my way carefully down the steps leading to Platform 14 and the train to Glasgow, then darted across the concourse, ignoring the angry comments of an irate taxi driver who had to brake sharply to avoid me. Crowds thronged the concourse: even in winter, Edinburgh was busy with tourists.

In spite of all my efforts, I was too late. As I briefly flashed my ticket at the collector standing by the barrier, the whistle blew and the train began slowly to slide off down the track.

'Damn,' I said, trying to catch my breath. Glancing up at the last carriage, I suddenly caught a glimpse of a face I recognised. Where had I seen that man before?

For a moment it was as though my heart had stopped. He was older certainly than when I last saw him, but there was no mistaking that profile.

Even after all the time that had passed and everything that had happened, I was sure it was Gabriel.

ONE

'You all right?' The ticket collector eyed me cautiously.

'Absolutely fine, thanks,' but my legs refused to support me and I collapsed on to the nearest bench.

He shook his head in disbelief. 'You shouldna be running for a train like that at your age, ye ken.' As this failed to elicit any response, he added in a kindly voice, 'There are plenty of trains to Glasgow.'

Still unable to speak, I nodded in agreement, rather put out at this mention of my age. 'I need some coffee,' I eventually managed to gasp.

He watched me through narrowed eyes as I lifted my briefcase and stood up slowly, testing my balance before walking over to the station buffet, trying to look calm and collected, but feeling neither. I hardly remember buying the coffee in the busy café-bar, but do recall perching on a high stool facing the wall to sip the scalding hot liquid.

A quick glance in one of the mock Art Deco mirrors lining the walls startled me. With my windswept fair hair, not to mention my pinched face drained of all colour, I looked positively ghoulish. It wasn't surprising the ticket collector had been alarmed.

I skimmed the froth off my cappuccino and ate it absentmindedly from the spoon, determined to reason with myself about what I'd seen, or thought I'd seen. Perhaps it was some trick of the light? At this time of year the artificial light casts long shadows: it all happened so long ago, that business with Gabriel.

My thoughts drifted back to the car accident. The trauma of that night had affected me badly, caused me to forget so much. But I'd been so very young then: surely after all these years I'd recovered? Or were there memories as yet unlocked, still lurking somewhere, come back to frighten me?

There was tightness at my heart that wouldn't go away no matter how hard I tried to talk myself round, tell myself it had all been a mistake. The man on the train was Gabriel.

'You finished with that cup?' The abrupt question from the surly waitress broke in on my confused thoughts as she hovered over me, extending a nail-bitten hand.

'Yes, yes,' I said without thinking, and pushed the half-empty cup towards her before glancing at my watch. While I'd been lost in thought, time had slipped away.

I jumped off the stool, scrabbling for my handbag and my briefcase and had to hurry again, luckily catching the next train with a minute to spare by the station clock. I eased myself into a corner seat, hoping not to be trapped by some chatty old lady eager to tell me about her shopping trip to Princes Street, but fortunately the sleek young man next to me buried his head in some complex report which appeared from a brief glimpse to consist of column after column of boring figures.

The train journey to Glasgow seemed to take forever and as I gazed out of the window watching darkness fall over the familiar landscape, my mind raced from one jumbled thought to another. I shut my eyes for a moment, trying to recall the details of Gabriel's face, but was too agitated to focus, kept seeing his face dissolve into the faces of the others who'd lived in that house in Hampstead all those years ago.

If only I could remember exactly what had happened. Had I chosen, deliberately or not, to let some memories stay buried? If so, there must be a good reason.

When I opened my eyes the woman opposite me was looking at me strangely and, although I responded with what was intended as a reassuring smile, she quickly retreated behind her copy of the *Edinburgh Evening News*.

By way of cover, I pulled my notebook from my bag and pretended to be engrossed, but that was soon abandoned in favour of again gazing out of the window. In the fading light my worried face reflected back at me in the glass.

At that time of day crowds of noisy schoolchildren crammed the carriages and it was a relief when many of them tumbled off at Falkirk, whooping and yelling as they disappeared into the frosty evening.

There were other problems to think about. My husband Simon, who works in further education, was concerned about his job and, by extension, so was I. My current part-time teaching job was quite enough to cope with and, in spite of several offers, I'd no intention of taking up a full-time post.

As if this wasn't enough, our younger daughter Deborah was threatening to abandon her Art College course and come home, a situation I could do nothing to resolve.

It was completely dark when we pulled into Queen Street station in Glasgow. I turned up my collar against the cold, crossed over the main station and jostled my way through the rush hour crowds to the suburban railway line, pausing only to buy an evening paper from the street vendor beside the station.

The hall clock was striking the hour as I turned the key in the lock. On Fridays Simon goes out to the pub after work with some of his department: "stress relief" he calls it, and he wouldn't be home for a good hour. I tugged off my boots (what bliss to be rid of them at last) and dropped my coat on the nearest chair.

'You'll have to wait,' I said to Motley the cat as he came purring round looking for his tea. Huffed at this lack of attention, he began to miaow loudly.

As he's a good few pounds overweight, Motley is on a diet, which doesn't put him in the best of tempers, but   much as I sympathised with his plight, I ignored him and ran upstairs. His *Weighless Cat Cuisine* could wait till later. What I had to do was far more urgent. It had to be somewhere in the house, I thought, quickly beginning to search.

For fifteen minutes I rummaged fruitlessly in my desk and the various boxes which serve as my excuse for a filing system, seriously hampered by Motley who had followed me upstairs and insisted on sitting down on anything I pulled out, refusing to budge no matter how many times he was shooed away.

Despairing of finding what I was after, and about to go downstairs to start making the meal, I suddenly thought about the glory hole that is the hall cupboard. After ten minutes of disciplined searching (it's so easy to be sidetracked) I found it, right at the back of a jumble of old programmes, postcards and assorted letters. It was one of several photos stuck between the pages of a souvenir programme for *Hair* at the Round House in Camden.

I lifted it out. The photos had been taken none too successfully with my very first Instamatic camera. There we were, frozen in time: all of us, smiling and relaxed and youthfully optimistic, though it was difficult to identify the exact location.

It was out of doors. Primrose Hill perhaps? A Sunday afternoon in summer? Impossible to tell who'd taken the picture, probably some passing stranger pressed into service for the occasion. It's the only photo where we're all together - Gabriel, Melanie, George, Josie, me - even Kara's there.

Apart from this, there was only one other photo of Gabriel: a drunken party in a dingy basement flat of some acquaintance or other. In those days, a party was a party, no matter how tenuous the connection to the host. It's hard to identify him among the crowd as no more than the merest glimpse of him is visible in a corner. He's partly blocked by someone's head, not to mention the smoke from the burning joss sticks.

But in this one, taken on that bright summer's day long ago, he was fully visible. His head was slightly inclined towards Melanie, so there was no mistaking that profile, the same face I'd seen on the train to Glasgow.

I sat back on my heels and stared at it, hardly conscious of time passing, tried to imagine myself back there on that summer's day, looking for any sign I might have made a mistake, scrutinising the photograph again, scanning every inch of it. The past stared back at me.

It was no use. There was no mistake. The car accident might have wiped much from my memory, but of this I was sure. The man on the train from Waverley was, without a doubt, Gabriel Santos.

Gabriel, who had been dead for over thirty years.

TWO

All night I tossed and turned, waking up drenched in sweat, falling asleep again, remembering fragments and strange combinations of events. Bits of memory drifted back into my consciousness, memories I thought lost forever.

I was back in London. Everyone was there: all those people who'd lived in that house in Hampstead. As with many dreams, things weren't quite right. Kara had abandoned the head to toe black she always wore and for some reason was dressed in bright red. With her long dark hair and olive complexion the outfit gave her an exotic, foreign look.

Worse still, on the edge of every dream there was Gabriel, languid, always watching, with us, yet not engaged in our activities. Those unsettling eyes, glistening like amber, that half smile that had so disturbed me, the look that said he knew something the rest of us didn't.

With a struggle I managed to pull myself out of the nightmares, where something soft and warm was attempting to smother me, to find to myself safe and sound in my own bed with Motley purring loudly beside me, swishing his tail over my face. I lay absolutely still for a moment, listening to the violent beating of my heart until gradually, very gradually, it slowed to a more regular rhythm. What was happening to me? Why should these memories begin to return after so long?

'Go away, Motley,' I said crossly, pushing him off the bed.

He sat on the floor, miaowing loudly at this unexpectedly harsh treatment before disappearing out of the door with an indignant swish of his tail.

I turned over, to find the space beside me empty. For a moment I was lost, then remembered it was Saturday and Simon had gone off to a conference at a hotel in Perth.

Bliss, a whole day to myself. Apart from a few bits and pieces of shopping I'd no plans: after such a sleepless night that suited me fine. I lay for a few moments, reluctant to go back to sleep, fearful the dreams might return. If this was going to be a pattern there was no way I'd cope, not knowing if they were dreams or real memories.

Everyone said how well I'd recovered from the accident, but now niggling doubts made me wonder if there were fragments of memory buried in the depths of my subconscious, locked away for some very good reason.

Shortly after nine o'clock I opted for a hot shower to chase away the last of the nightmares before going downstairs to prepare a leisurely breakfast of croissants and coffee. If I manage to stay off the goodies all week in the interests of my waistline, a treat at the weekend won't do any harm, or so I tried to convince myself.

I walked slowly downstairs to the kitchen, at the same time drying my hair with a towel and trying to avoid tripping over Motley who'd re-emerged in search of food. Like most cats he refuses to take the direct way down.

'Did Simon forget to feed you before he went out?' I asked, knowing full well that the attention he was giving me was cupboard love.

The sunlight was streaming in through the window, the dusting of shimmering frost on the grass in the back garden confirming it was really cold, but it was cosy enough indoors with the central heating set at high.

As I started to grind the beans for some real coffee, idly watching Motley devour the food in his bowl as if he hadn't been fed in weeks, the phone rang. An irrational feeling of panic seized me and I leaned over to switch off the grinder, before hesitantly lifting the receiver.

'Hello,' I said cautiously.

It was Simon. 'Alison, is that you? Hope I didn't wake you.' He sounded concerned.

'Good gracious, no. I've been up for ages,' I lied, trying to juggle the grinder, the coffee beans and the telephone.

'Are you okay?'

My tossing and turning during the night must have disturbed him, but hopefully I hadn't been talking in my sleep. From time to time guilt about the accident re-surfaces: he was at the wheel of the car when it happened, though it was in no way his fault.

'Sorry, Simon,' I said, 'only a nightmare. It must have been something to do with eating late last night.'

He said to someone in a low voice, 'I'll be along in a minute,' before adding to me, 'If the afternoon session looks boring, I'll come home early.'

I pictured him standing by the phone frowning and as he habitually did, running his fingers through his dark (well greying) hair, which makes it stand on end in a most alarming way.

'No, please don't, Simon,' I jumped in a bit too quickly and rang off with a hurried goodbye before he could make another offer about cutting short his day at the conference.

For a moment I stood looking at the silent telephone. Truth to tell, I wasn't quite sure everything was all right. And the worst of it was I didn't know why. 'Pull yourself together, Alison,' I said aloud. 'After all, it was only a dream.'

If only I hadn't seen that man on the train yesterday. I'd been so certain that part of my life was behind me, my time living in Kara's house in London a distant memory. Apparently not. And the more I thought about it, the odder it all seemed.

Admittedly, once I'd met Simon he'd occupied all my thoughts - and my time - and whatever was happening at Kara's became less and less of a concern.

Where had they all gone? Kara had died, that I'd heard, and the last time I'd passed the house, before we came back to Scotland, it had been empty and shuttered, the windows blank-eyed, the building neglected, unloved. In our rush to leave to leave and continue with our own lives we'd given little thought to those left behind.

Besides, I was more than a little anxious to leave the area where the accident had happened. It had all been so awful, so sudden. One minute we were driving down Hampstead High Street, chatting happily, the next we were trapped in the car, aware only that there had been some kind of collision. Simon had no more than a few scratches and though I wasn't seriously injured, for a brief moment I thought I was about to die before losing consciousness, the result of a blow to my head.

I didn't die of course, slowly regained my health, but not my memory, at least not entirely. There seemed to be little gaps, days and weeks missing and it had taken a long time before my confidence returned. I couldn't leave London quickly enough, hoping being back in my native city would complete my recovery.

Again and again I told myself there must have been some mistake about that man on the train, some lapse of memory, some imagining, triggered by who knows what. Gabriel was dead. He had no power any longer over anyone and it was nonsense to fret, trying to recall what was long past. It was simple. Something had happened, had reminded me of Gabriel and I'd made the association with the man on the Glasgow train. In that strange half-light of late afternoon at Waverley station it was all too easy for imagination to create strange shapes.

Yes, I told myself firmly, there was nothing to worry about. But a little niggling doubt wouldn't go away and no matter how hard I tried, I couldn't think of anything that might have prompted memories of Gabriel.

There was no point in going over and over the same ground or I'd be in no fit state to cope, so while the coffee brewed I went out into the porch to collect the morning paper and the mail.

Apart from the usual junk mail and the credit card statement which I immediately hid at the bottom of the pile (while trying to remember exactly what I'd used the card for the previous month), I saw with pleasure there was a letter from Maura, an unexpected treat as she usually prefers to phone or email.

I carried everything back through to the kitchen and sat down at the table to read the newspaper during breakfast.

After two cups of coffee and two croissants, liberally spread with butter and apricot jam (there's no sense in half measures), my fears had all but disappeared. Having justified to myself a third cup of coffee with the explanation that after my restless night the caffeine kick was badly needed, I settled down to read the letter.

Maura is our oldest child. I miss her since she went to work in London recently, but she keeps in touch and amuses us with her stories of life in the big city. Deborah and Alastair both live in Glasgow.

We see a lot of Deborah and very little of Alastair who is the classic academic, dedicated to his research project, but alarmingly vague in all other areas of life.

As I tore open the bulky envelope haphazardly in pleasurable anticipation (we have a paper knife somewhere) a folded piece of newspaper fell out. Intrigued, I picked it up from the floor and smoothed out her letter.

'Dear Mum, (Maura had written)

You'll never guess? *The Hampstead and Highgate Express* is running a series on local mysteries of the past and this was the one they published last week.'

What had Maura found that would be of interest to me?

'I only noticed it really because of the address. Wasn't that where you used to live?

I guess it all happened about the time you were there. Why have you never mentioned it?'

I put the letter to one side and after a moment's hesitation unfolded the newspaper with trembling hands and spread it out on the kitchen table.

MYSTERY DROWNING IN HAMPSTEAD POND, said the headline, and immediately below was a very grainy, but still recognisable, black and white photo of Gabriel as I'd known him all those years ago.

THREE

'Simon,' I said, flicking through a magazine in an attempt to appear only vaguely interested in the reply, 'do you remember a man called Gabriel Santos?'

It was later that evening and I'd spent several agonising hours wondering how to introduce this topic, unable to stop thinking about the newspaper article Maura had sent.

Thoroughly confused about what I'd seen, or more probably imagined, I'd absolutely no idea how to find out the truth about Gabriel. When you assume someone is dead - no, correction, when you know someone is dead - the last thing you expect is to see them on a train from Edinburgh. Hadn't Kara identified the body? She wouldn't have made that kind of mistake, especially after all that had happened.

Was it too convenient he'd died when he did? None of us had seen him when they'd pulled him out of the pond on Hampstead Heath. We'd been happy to leave that to Kara. Now she too was long dead, and there was no way of finding out the truth.

Simon had come home early. The conference had turned out to be as uninspiring as he'd predicted, but by then I was trawling the counters of the shops in Argyle Street on a pre-Christmas shopping expedition. Anything to distract me from returning thoughts of Gabriel.

Being a caring wife I waited till we'd had dinner - courtesy of the local supermarket, with the excuse of being too tired to cook. Perhaps beginning the conversation in the middle of the football highlights wasn't a good idea. It was clear I didn't have his undivided attention.

'When we were in London, do you recall meeting a man called Gabriel Santos?' I repeated.

He turned from the television set and looked at me in a strange way, as if he didn't quite understand. Probably his mind was still on the sports programme.

'Who did you say?' The abruptness of his tone took me by surprise.

'Nothing: it doesn't matter.' Why was I pursuing this madness?

'No, no, what did you say?' That same edge to his voice.

I shrugged, now trying to sound suitably vague. 'I was thinking: do you remember Gabriel Santos?' Then adding, to help jog his memory, 'He'd been one of the tenants in Kara's house before I arrived, and then he came back while I was living there.'

Was it my imagination at work again or was there a moment's hesitation before he replied, avoiding my gaze, 'Good Lord, Alison, that was ages ago. I can't possibly remember all the people I've met over the years.'

He turned back to the television, making it plain he wasn't keen to pursue what he thought was a foolish question, particularly when there was football to engage his attention.

Having started again, I was persistent, determined to have an answer.

'You must have some memory of him. It was that Spring when we first met. When I had that room in Kara's place.'

He's really very kind at heart my husband, particularly when he realises it's something important to me. But football is football.

'Yes, I certainly do remember meeting you, Alison, but maybe we could leave this conversation until the game's finished?'

He turned once more to the television, in time to miss a goal. Oops, better to do as he suggested and beat a hasty retreat to the kitchen to make some coffee.

Ten minutes later he came in so quietly I didn't hear him and jumped in alarm when he put his arms around my waist.

'Careful,' I said, almost dropping the coffee cup.

'You see what it's like to be distracted in the middle of something,' he grinned.

'Oh, you're hopeless,' I replied, kissing him.

We sat at the kitchen table with our coffee, neither of us talking, not yet. I'd asked my question, and now waited for Simon to reply.

He put his cup down.

'What was that you were asking me about someone we knew when we were in London?'

There was something vaguely disturbing in the way he said this, but I couldn't think what it might be. Perhaps he was still upset about the missed goal.

'Do you recall Gabriel Santos? Remember how he came back to Kara's during the time I'd a room there? He'd been one of the original tenants from what the others said, but he'd left, gone off somewhere as people tended to do in those days.'

He chewed thoughtfully for a moment or two before replying very matter-of–factly, 'Wasn't he that bloke who drowned? Something to do with that girl who stayed there? Jennifer? No, Melanie, wasn't it? Wasn't it all something to do with her?'

'Yes, of course, that was the connection.'

How had I forgotten that, forgotten about Melanie? Not wanting to miss this opportunity to jog his memory I went on quickly, 'What I want to know is if you would recognise him again?'

His face was expressionless as he said, 'Hardly likely, Alison, since I expect one skeleton looks very like another. Not that I've been asked that question before.'

He chuckled, amused at his own wit, and gulped down a mouthful of coffee, then put the cup down abruptly, spilling a little on the saucer.

'What's all this about anyway? Why this sudden interest in the past? You're not having problems again, are you? I knew those nightmares were a sign…'

I shook my head, interrupting him.

'No, nothing like that. I'm feeling fine, you'll be glad to hear.'

He seemed to breathe a sigh of relief.

'Thank goodness. Please don't do that, Alison, it frightens me.' He went back to drinking his coffee.

His next remark worried me even more.

'The past is past, Alison. We've enough to do managing the present. Leave it.'

If I hadn't known better, I'd have thought he was warning me, and decided to drop the subject, didn't even mention the letter from Maura, though I couldn't say why.

What could I have told him that didn't sound silly or hysterical? That I saw someone who might or might not have been Gabriel Santos on the train from Edinburgh?

Simon would say what any sensible person would: it was someone who looked like Gabriel or was no more than a trick of the light.

But forgetting was easier said than done, though I'd made a pretty good job of that so far, it would seem.

What had happened was perfectly clear to me. In spite of all the doctors had said at the time, my memory hadn't completely returned and some events still lay buried deep, events that for some reason I couldn't or wouldn't remember.

Whether it really was Gabriel or only someone who looked like him, I was beginning to glimpse slivers of the past and wouldn't be able to rest until I found out the truth. Was whatever happened in Kara's house to come back and haunt me after all this time?

This conversation with Simon was pointless. He didn't want to discuss the past, and there and then I decided not to involve him any further. The decision wasn't an easy one, as over the years we've shared most of our problems. But not this.

Later, when we were going up to bed, he said again, 'What brought all that back, Alison? Those questions about that man…what was he called…Gabriel Santos?'

I shook my head. 'It's nothing, nothing at all.' There was no way he could know what had happened all those years ago at Kara's. I only knew part of the story myself, but was more determined than ever to find out exactly what secrets remained hidden. That's if there were any secrets. 'I came across an old photo yesterday while clearing out the hall cupboard.'

Simon gave me a bewildered look, since my preferred method with cupboards is cramming in as much as possible rather than clearing them out, but all he did was shrug.

'Suit yourself.'

It wasn't an entirely true account of what had happened: already little lies were beginning to weave themselves into the fabric of events.

Afterwards I bitterly regretted I hadn't made him listen to me, hadn't told him the whole truth about my suspicions. But by then it was too late.

Fragments of memory began to disturb my days and my nights as I became more and more convinced it had been Gabriel on the train.

To make matters worse, a few days before Christmas I saw Gabriel again. And in a way I'd never have expected.

FOUR

The strong scent of rosemary started it, triggered the memory: pungent and aromatic, it was the smell of Kara's kitchen.

Early morning, the morning of my birthday and there I was perched half way up the ladder in the kitchen. After another sleepless night, I'd finally wakened with a start about five o'clock, lying for a while staring at the ceiling, listening to the regular rhythm of Simon's breathing.

After counting the roses on the border round the bedroom wall for the umpteenth time I slid quietly out of bed, drawing my dressing gown around me. The central heating hadn't yet clicked on and the house was decidedly chilly.

The low cupboards were easy but I had to perch precariously on the top step of the ladder to reach the very back of the tall larder unit, a dangerous position made even worse by Motley deciding to join me. Delighted to have the unexpected pleasure of company this early in the morning, he'd climbed up the ladder behind me, then sat down half way to groom himself.

Packet after packet was discarded into the large black bag secured on the handle of one of the cupboards as I wondered how it was possible to have missed so many out-of-date reminders. As I stretched on tiptoe to lift down the packets crammed in the corner, a strong aroma of rosemary hit me and immediately a picture flashed into my mind. This was the smell of Kara's kitchen and so strong was the scent, it was as though I was back there. Shaking uncontrollably, I came down the ladder extra carefully, abruptly dislodging Motley in the process.

Hugely annoyed, he jumped to the floor, swishing his tail, miaowing his way out of the room. I sat down with a bump at the kitchen table, forcing myself to breathe deeply to restore my thoughts, to stop my heart from racing.

With my eyes tightly shut, I willed the memory to disappear, but it had the opposite effect. Bit by bit memories of that early Spring evening in Kara's kitchen, that calm evening disturbed by Gabriel, slowly returned.

We were all there: Josie, Melanie and George and even Kara. It must have been late afternoon, because the light was on, though it wasn't yet entirely dark, and the kitchen, in the basement of the house, was always gloomy, even in the middle of summer.

We were having a meal together (a rare event) so we must have been celebrating something but, try as I might to remember, no reason for the occasion came to mind. What I could recall was the air heavy with the tang of roast lamb and some other unfamiliar aroma.

'What's making the lamb smell so delicious?' I asked Melanie in all innocence.

She looked at me through narrowed eyes, to check this wasn't a tease.

'Why rosemary of course, rosemary for remembrance. I thought you were educated. Don't you know your Shakespeare?'

I blushed but said nothing. The lines from *Hamlet* were certainly familiar to me, having recently studied the text at school, but I'd no idea what rosemary smelled like. My mother, trained by the severe shortages of the war, believed in the good old-fashioned cooking method of boiling meat till all the flavour had gone.

'Oh, leave her in peace, Melanie,' said Kara indulgently.

Kara was swaying backwards and forwards in the rocking chair in the corner, from time to time taking a drag on one of the small black cheroots she favoured. One of the many cats that roamed the flat - a tortoiseshell I recall - purred contentedly on her knee.

There was a lot of chatter and laughter as we tried to work in the kitchen without bumping into each other.

'A case of "too many cooks" I think,' muttered Josie as she and Melanie collided again.

Although Kara's kitchen was one of those large rooms, full of the nooks and crannies you'd expect in a Victorian villa, most of the space was taken up by an enormous, battered old table and junk shops chairs. On the far wall a cumbersome mahogany dresser, crammed with an assortment of mismatched china, brooded over everything.

As usual, George was giving plenty of advice, but doing nothing.

'This is all looking a bit dangerous. Don't you think it would be better if you agreed who was doing what and stuck to it?' was his languid contribution to the proceedings from the depths of his comfortable chair.

Finally Melanie lifted a cushion and threw it at him. Fortunately her aim was good and she hit him fair and square else it might have landed on one of the pots simmering on the cooker.

'Oh, do shut up, George,' she said crossly. 'Why don't you make yourself useful instead of sitting there criticising?'

Undisturbed by her comments, George grinned. Yet another occasion when I guessed his dark good looks made him think he could get away with anything as far as women were concerned.

'I was helping. That's what I'm good at, organising people,' he complained. 'Anyway,' he added, 'I thought I was helping by keeping out of everyone's way and letting you all get on with it.'

This was so near the mark I had to turn away to hide my laughter while Josie, determined to defend him, thrust a bundle of knives and forks into his hands.

'Here, George, you can at least lay the table. That will test your organisational skills.'

George rose with a sigh, pushed back his floppy hair and began his allotted task without another word. He had so much hair, more even than was fashionable at the time, curling down his neck, gypsy fashion. All he lacked was the earring.

He smiled to himself as he began to lay out knives and forks with an apparent good grace, but proceeded to do it in a deliberately clumsy way, knocking loudly into everything and everyone as he made his way round, much to Melanie's annoyance.

When the table was laid after a fashion, George sat down on the low stool beside Kara's chair with a self-satisfied air and abruptly dislodged the tortoiseshell from her knee.

Absentmindedly, she began stroking his hair, as though he were one of the cats. Somehow it made me feel uncomfortable and I turned my head away quickly so that they were out of my line of sight. It wasn't that there was anything overtly sexual in their behaviour, at least I didn't think so at the time, but it was unexpected.

This behaviour upset Josie though, and I could see her watching them both all the time as she moved round the kitchen, deliberately banging pots onto the cooker.

Melanie stopped what she was doing and said crossly, 'Hey, careful there. You'll scald yourself if you carry on like that.'

Josie went bright red and mumbled something I didn't quite catch in reply, but she started to move about more quietly, carefully avoiding looking at anyone, and for a moment it seemed she was about to burst into tears. Or it might have been no more than the steam from the cooking had misted up her glasses. She was no natural beauty, but she did nothing to help herself, apparently unaware of her long lank hair and those thick glasses, unflattering to the round shape of her face.

Out of the corner of my eye I caught Melanie looking over towards George and saw Kara shake her head ever so slightly. It was only the merest movement, almost undetectable, but George immediately rose and went over to look out of the heavily barred window overlooking the front yard, whistling tunelessly as he did so.

'Oh, for goodness sake, George, can you stop that noise? It's awful.' Melanie sounded crosser than ever.

Now it was George's turn to look upset.

'Don't you know that I had music lessons in one of the best public schools in England?'

This remark was so silly it made us all laugh, even George, and I breathed a sigh of relief. Another disaster avoided - and now we could continue with the meal.

Kara transferred her affection back to the cat which had resumed its position on her knee, much to its delight, and it began to purr loudly while I went on making the salad, trying to pretend none of this was happening.

In an atmosphere of calm and friendship we'd almost finished the first course, a soup Melanie had made from a recipe she'd found in *NOVA* magazine, when Gabriel came in.

No, back a step. It's important to describe this accurately, to freeze the memory. One minute he wasn't in the kitchen and the next he seemed to fill the whole space. He made a habit of that: coming into a room so quietly that you suddenly looked up to find him there right beside you, like one of Kara's cats, soft footed and watchful.

The idle chatter died away as though the temperature in the room had suddenly dropped.

He leaned against the doorpost and surveyed the scene before him. His eyes, the colour of oloroso sherry, narrowed to slits as he looked round at us all.

What did I remember about him? His tall, lean frame, his dark skin and eyes, his curious lopsided smile that was almost a sneer. And those long elegant hands which for some reason sent a shiver up my spine.

It wasn't that he was handsome: not in a conventional way. His eyes were too close together, his chin too pointed, yet he was hopelessly compelling. 'Don't let me interrupt your little party,' he said.

In the half shadow of the doorway he looked more than a little menacing. 'I'm sure you're all having a great time.' His voice had an underlying foreign accent, one I couldn't quite place.

As though on command, we all stopped eating. There was a long silence, broken only by the loud ticking of the ancient clock on the wall and, though I looked at the others for guidance, no one spoke.

He stood there, totally still, watching, completely at ease with himself, obviously amused at his effect on the rest of us. Then suddenly he made a move, came right into the room and crossed over to the chair where Kara had been sitting.

The cat, which had taken up a comfortable position on the chair as soon as Kara had vacated it, was swept off. No one protested, though there would have been an outcry if anyone else had attempted this with one of Kara's cats.

Gabriel settled into Kara's chair and looked round, well aware of the effect he'd created. Even at this distance in time, there was no escaping the air of menace his presence brought.

That was the beginning of it all.

FIVE

No-one spoke, then suddenly everyone moved at once: Josie shuffled uncomfortably in her chair, Melanie, almost in defiance, lifted her spoon and went on eating her soup and I nervously copied her example.

Melanie looked up at him, her eyes troubled. 'You're welcome to join us, Gabriel,' she said in a low voice. 'Pull up a chair. There's plenty of food. I think we've made enough to feed an army.' The words tumbled out, a sign of her disquiet.

Kara said nothing, made no gesture. Why not? How strange that seems now. It was her house after all.

At that moment I turned my head, and saw her looking at him with what can only be described as hatred. None of the others seemed to have noticed: they were all too busy gazing, as though mesmerised, at Gabriel.

He waved his hand dismissively. 'I've eaten already,' was all he said.

He began rocking backwards and forwards, slowly at first and then with a persistent rhythm that was most upsetting. All the time he was humming to himself, ever so quietly.

The tune meant nothing to me at the time, but Kara must have recognised it because she became more and more agitated, so much so I was convinced he was doing this deliberately, trying to upset her.

Kara had tackled the first course with an enthusiasm unusual for her, but when the lamb was served up, she did no more than pick at it, pushing it round her plate in a way that convinced no one. Every now and then she would look over at Gabriel, her face expressionless as a mask.

It was all so normal, so calm once again, a little niggle of doubt made me wonder if I'd been imagining it all. If Gabriel was aware of the tension he'd caused, he didn't show it. But then you could never guess anything Gabriel thought. He'd only been back at Kara's less than a month, but his arrival had changed everything.

There was a sense he and Kara were each aware the other was in the room, as if there was a current of electricity sparking between them.

Gabriel continued rocking, continued humming, sitting back totally relaxed, his eyes tightly shut. The longer I listened, the more familiar the tune seemed, though I couldn't place it, didn't find out what it was until much later. In a way it was another example of how totally, how utterly, self-absorbed he was.

The meal was spoiled. The spontaneous gaiety had gone, leaving us deflated. Nothing was said, but we could all feel the change.

The only person seemingly oblivious to this tense atmosphere was George, who devoured everything on his plate. 'No one else hungry?' he asked between mouthfuls, scraping the last of the vegetables onto his plate from the serving dish. 'You do all have poor appetites, you lot. Still you do enjoy food all the more when you've had a hand in the preparations.'

No one, not even Melanie, bothered to contradict him, though normally a remark like that from lazy George would have provoked a good-natured outcry.

He munched on contentedly while the rest of us toyed with our food in silence. He was the only one who had any appetite for the dessert of crème brûlée lovingly prepared by Josie because she knew how much George liked it. It lay there, its caramelised topping scenting the air as it cooled.

George made do with one helping though he did say, 'I'd better leave some of this for you guys to have later,' as he looked hopefully round the table, clearly willing one of us to coax him to a second helping, but no one was in the mood for these games. He sighed in resignation, his boyish looks giving him an air of injured innocence.

Josie pushed away her untouched plate.

'I'll skip the coffee,' she said very quietly, as Melanie stood up and went over to the sink to fill the kettle.

Kara also got to her feet, leaning over to stub out her cheroot in the overflowing ashtray on the windowsill.

Gabriel, who had appeared totally detached from all that was going on around him, and hadn't said a word the entire time, now slowly opened his eyes and uncoiled himself lazily from the rocking chair. He yawned and stretched himself up to his full height, reminding me more of a cat than ever.

'I would like some coffee, little Melanie,' he said, moving slowly to stand so close behind her his breath stirred little tendrils of her hair.

I could see Melanie's back stiffen. 'No problem, Gabriel,' she replied in a tight little voice, quite unlike her normal tone. 'If you'd let me pass to put the kettle on.'

He made a mocking little flourish of standing aside, but only a little bit, so that she still had to squeeze between him and the table to reach the cooker.

Kara's face had gone white, her expression blank. It was as though she had buttoned herself up, afraid she had already given away too much.

Was that when it all began? Sitting at my own kitchen table with my eyes tight shut I could remember so much, but only so much. It was as though my memory was returning, but in little snapshots.

Josie at the table looking warily at everyone; George picking at the remains of the lamb on the dresser, where it had grown cold and congealed; Kara at the doorway, not wanting to stay, but reluctant to leave. And Gabriel close behind Melanie, not touching her, but caressing her with his breath, giving her no escape.

After that, it seemed that wherever Melanie was, Gabriel was somewhere nearby, and Kara withdrew increasingly into herself, so that she hardly ever came out to the pub with us anymore.

It was as though he enjoyed mocking us all, enjoyed making us feel uncomfortable. It was all a game to him.

But not to Kara. When you went to see her, knocked at the door of her room, there was no reply, yet you knew she was in there, sitting in the dark, not responding.

It was with mounting horror I remembered it wasn't long after that episode in the kitchen that Kara had made her suicide attempt.

SIX

It was only by chance I was in the cupboard that day. Officially it's the school audio-visual room, but being tiny and without windows most of us refer to it as "the cupboard." Probably totally illegal now, under some European directive or other, but we're so short of accommodation in Strathelder High we have to make do.

The few weeks before we break up for Christmas are the most difficult of the year. School parties and discos are the only topics of conversation and the pupils, even those who consider themselves very grown up, become more and more excited as the end of term approaches.

The result is stressed-out teachers, desperately trying to find something to amuse their restless students, a task not easy in the age of electronic gadgetry. I hoped there just might be something to interest them here among the piles of videos.

There had been no more stirrings of memory since that dreadful one in the kitchen on the morning of my birthday, but most nights sleep eluded me and from time to time I caught Simon giving me a sideways glance, as though he suspected something was wrong. Tempted as I was to confide in him, the right opportunity didn't present itself. Besides, I'd almost convinced myself if I didn't talk about it, didn't think about it, it would have no reality.

And what are ghosts if you refuse to believe in them? Nothing. Even if I did have to resign myself to living with that uncomfortable nagging, this constant itch, at the back of my mind.

Unfortunately, I'd had one or two frights in the meantime. The worst was the previous week while shopping in Fraser's department store in Glasgow.

Having managed to track down the shade of blue jumper my mother wanted for Christmas, I was feeling very pleased. She hadn't asked outright, but her hints had been of the strongest kind and she'd almost directed me to the exact rack in the store.

Rather than wait for the lift, I decided to take the stairs. As I started to make my way down that plush sweeping staircase, all deep red carpets and wood so highly polished it reflects your image, I happened to glance over to the entrance to the lift in the far corner. I stopped suddenly, almost causing an elderly woman behind me to stumble.

'I'm so sorry,' I apologised as she glared at me.

My heart was thudding loudly. It was only a back view, but surely it was Gabriel standing there, among the small crowd waiting for the lift to arrive?

Determined not to make a spectacle of myself by fainting, I clutched at the banisters for support and crept down the last few steps. What to do? Sidle off or confront him?

Don't be stupid, I told myself firmly, this could be the opportunity you've been waiting for. Trying to think of an opening gambit, I headed towards him, past the cosmetic counters, all the time moving this way and that for a better view. Unfortunately at one of the cosmetic counters a very glamorous young lady was selling some new beauty product and wrongly guessed she had a customer, though goodness knows I probably looked as if I could do with some help.

She clicked over towards me on her impossibly high heels, a bright smile fixed on her face. She was young, but the amount of makeup she was wearing gave her face a strange mask-like appearance.

'Is madam interested in our new range of cleansing products, especially designed for the more mature skin...,' she began smoothly.

As I stared at her, she paused in mid flow, retreated hastily and began to fumble with the various items displayed on the counter in gaudy shades of bright pink and gold.

The man was still standing by the lift. If only he would turn round and let me have a better view. My feet felt like lead as I crossed the floor: only a few yards, but it seemed like miles. Screwing up my courage, I took a deep breath and came right up behind him to tap him tentatively on the shoulder. He turned round, a look of surprise on his face, and to my horror I realised he most definitely wasn't Gabriel.

He gazed at me in some concern, as well he might.

'Sorry, sorry,' I stammered. 'I thought you were someone else.'

He smiled, but it was clear he didn't believe me. Flushed with embarrassment, I kept repeating, 'I'm sorry,' over and over again until suddenly the lift doors opened.

'I really have to go, you know,' he said gently.

'Of course, of course, many apologies again.'

He went into the lift but continued to look at me with a puzzled expression until finally the doors closed and he was, much to my relief, whisked away.

By this time, worn out from the experience and from making so many apologies, the shopping trip was abandoned and I made for home.

Apart from imagined sightings, I coped. The more often I "saw" Gabriel and was proved wrong, the more I felt reassured.

As the memory of the incident in Fraser's faded, I became more convinced that the man on the train couldn't have been

Gabriel. And even if it was, what could be done about events that happened so many years ago?

Once I'd made this decision to put it all to the back of my mind I felt almost cheerful, and began to look forward to Christmas. In spite of all the chaos in school I was in a much more relaxed and sunny mood as I went along to the cupboard that day, deep in thought about what to select.

The audio-visual cupboard was set up to allow you to preview any tapes you might want to use with your class, but because it's such a small place, you couldn't help but become involved in whatever else was going on.

That afternoon, Harry Sneddon, the History teacher, was there already. My final decision was to try a video of *Julius Caesar* in an attempt to stir some signs of interest in my fourth years. Without much hope of success: at that stage, their favourite word is "boring" and nothing bores them more than Shakespeare.

Harry was browsing through the videos in the History section, only pausing now and again to push back his thatch of white hair that kept flopping over his face and obscuring his view.

He's a taciturn person, not much given to idle chit chat, and I was relieved when my friend Susie Littlejohn, who is also a Guidance teacher, breezed into the room.

As Susie is small and plump, it was going to be a tight squeeze. Susie hates silence, so with a general, 'Hello, room for one more?' to both of us she asked Harry by way of conversation, 'Trying to find something to keep them amused, are you, Harry?'

He looked up glumly from his notepad.

'I'm looking for material for the third years for next term. Something to keep them busy while I'm off on one of these refresher courses and some other poor soul has to take them.'

This was a long speech for him and Susie regarded him with astonishment.

'What kind of refresher course? I thought you were due to retire within the next couple of years.'

Harry, who had brightened at the prospect of someone else teaching his classes, looked glum again.

'I had applied for early retirement, but that's all up in the air now. Apparently the education department has run out of money. So that's why I'm going on this course.'

It was hard to follow the logic of this, but then I've long since ceased to understand the bureaucratic workings of the education department.

He held up the video box he was examining.

'Seen any of this series, have you? Just yesterday to me, but ancient history to the third years.'

I was about to mutter to Susie, 'Well, of course the 1960s would be ancient history to teenagers, who consider anyone over thirty is on their last legs,' when I suddenly caught sight of the box and was seized by a totally irrational feeling of panic. The box Harry was holding up was quite clearly labelled *Memories of 1968*.

As I turned away and breathed deeply to calm my racing heart, I was aware of Susie, who misses nothing, eyeing me suspiciously. In spite of my attempts at smiling to cover my fear, it was clear from her expression she sensed something was wrong. She's not a Guidance teacher for nothing.

'Of course,' Harry went on, pushing back his hair again and blissfully unaware of my distress, 'there's a good range of these available now. I mean you probably remember all of this, girls.'

Susie was too busy watching me to respond to Harry's very non-PC use of the word "girls".

Just my luck Susie had come into the room at all. We've been friends for years since we met at teacher training college and she knows me well: too well at times. I was in no mood for trying to disguise my concern, but had to see what it was Harry had found on the video.

Buoyed up by the fact he wouldn't actually have to teach any of this, Harry had become almost talkative. He pressed the button on the video as I waited with some apprehension to see what would appear on the screen.

'The swinging '60s, eh?' he chuckled.

A feeling of relief swept over me almost as soon as the film started. Harry was panning through the footage of the Paris street riots of May 1968 when the students from the Sorbonne, a collection of Marxists, Trotskyites and dissidents of every allegiance, laid siege to Paris in an attempt to bring down the government. Nothing to do with me there. I didn't arrive in London till later, so my panic was no more than a symptom of my current general unease.

I continued to watch, partly out of politeness and partly out of genuine interest. A moment later, a few frames further on, and I felt my heart lurch.

'Stop the video, stop it right there,' I shouted, 'no, back a bit, that's it, at that bit.'

Harry was so surprised he immediately did as I asked. 'Gosh, Alison, what's wrong? You look as if you've seen a ghost.' He gazed at me, his finger poised over the re-wind button.

Out of the corner of my eye I caught sight of Susie standing staring at me, her mouth open in surprise, but I was past caring.

My fleeting impression had not been mistaken. The frozen image stared back at me. His head was back, his mouth open as if he were shouting. There at the front of the heaving, shouting mob on the Rive Gauche was Gabriel.

'Are you all right, Alison?' asked Harry, clearly alarmed by my excited behaviour.

'What date was that? I mean, what was the exact date of the film?' The words tumbled out.

Harry blustered, confused by this sudden turn of events. 'I didn't realise you were so interested in modern history...' His voice tailed off as he saw the fierce look on my face and he busied himself studying the cover of the box.

He said, 'May 10th, 1968, as far as I can tell,' pointing to the information on the back of the box. I checked for myself, then made him play the sequence through once more, not daring to look towards Susie, who'd remained strangely quiet while all this was going on.

Not a man usually given to curiosity, Harry was clearly desperate to ask me what all this was about, but I ignored his unspoken question. I hadn't been mistaken this time. There in that mob, encouraging others on, was Gabriel. Even if I'd imagined the whole episode of seeing him on the train I was absolutely certain it was Gabriel in this footage.

What on earth was Gabriel doing in Paris at those student riots in 1968 when, as far as I knew, he'd been living in Kara's house? Was he a student then? I'd no idea.

Susie suddenly sprang into life, grasped me firmly by the arm and with a quick, 'Thanks Harry,' steered me out of the room.

Too weak and drained to make any show of resistance, I followed her out, still trying to make sense of the video clip. Once outside in the corridor, Susie pulled me round to face her.

'Now, Alison, will you tell me what's going on?'

SEVEN

Overcome by a sudden faintness, I leaned against the wall for support.

'Not here, Susie.'

She wasn't to be shaken off so easily and in a tone of voice not to be argued with she said, 'It's nearly lunchtime. Let's go across the road to Gina's café. It's too early for anyone from school to be there.'

Once she'd settled me in one of the booths (which judging by the Formica topped tables hadn't been changed since the 1950s) with a large cappuccino and one of Gina's famous diet-breaking doughnuts, she folded her arms on the table and looked across at me expectantly.

'Well?'

I was reluctant to start, needed to gather my thoughts, decide how much to tell her. I stirred and stirred my coffee until she said impatiently, 'Are you going to drink that or go on until it's completely cold?'

Spoon in mid-air, I hesitated before saying, 'I'm thinking, Susie, thinking where to begin.' A deep breath and then, 'If you wanted to find someone, where would you start?'

She lifted her eyebrows in mock horror. 'Well, that depends, Alison, on whether you're looking for a new husband or a lover? Though I must say I thought you and Simon were getting along fine.'

'Don't be silly,' I said through a mouthful of doughnut, her attempt at humour already lifting my spirits.

'Well then, be a bit more specific. Who is it you're looking for exactly?'

She cocked her head to one side, a habit that made her look even more birdlike than usual.

But now I'd decided to confide in her I'd little idea where to begin. How much did I remember from so long ago and how much was overlaid by what happened afterwards, by what others had told me?

Susie prompted me.

'Is it that old car accident? Problems again dealing with memories?'

'No, at least I don't think so,' I whispered.

'But it is something to do with that time you spent in London years ago, isn't it? Ah, something's happened to upset you?'

I nodded, not yet trusting myself to speak, afraid of bursting into tears.

She said in a softer voice, 'It's perfectly clear something's troubling you. You haven't been your usual self for weeks, so why don't you tell me what's the matter?'

As I made no reply, but went back to stirring my coffee, she laid her hand over mine to stop me.

'Alison, believe me, even talking about it will help.'

If I couldn't trust Susie who could I trust, so with some reluctance, and mostly because I couldn't think of a plausible cover story on the spur of the moment, I told her about my sighting of Gabriel on the train. I recalled my wavering between certainty and disbelief, my reading of the article that Maura had sent and how it been the cause of my reaction to the video we'd seen.

This was a very abridged version, and at first the look on her face said she wasn't convinced my story had been enough to cause such a violent reaction. But as I continued, filling in the details, Susie began to eat more slowly until she stopped altogether, her fork poised in mid-air. She tugged at one of her dangling silver earrings, something she does when particularly concerned.

'You may or may not have seen this Gabriel,' she said slowly, 'but if you didn't see him something must have triggered a memory of him. An incident you've tried hard to suppress has surfaced after all these years. Relax and try to describe what you remember about being there: any small thing that could have set all this off.'

I closed my eyes and again tried to visualise myself back in that house in Hampstead, hoping if I let my memory function in a random way, rather than trying to remember the events in sequence, it would help. In spite of several minutes of concentration nothing useful came to mind.

'Why you were there?'' urged Susie impatiently, possibly concerned I might stop in the middle of my tale.

'The usual story: I went to London instead of straight to university because of a broken romance. Jamie, I think his name was.' I laughed bitterly and said, 'To think how upset I was at the time and now can scarcely remember what he looked like. Whereas Gabriel, well, how could I forget him?'

Susie leaned over the table eagerly, encouraging me to continue.

'Go on, there must be more to it than that. What happened?'

This was getting in deeper than I wanted, even if Susie was a really good friend, but it was too late now.

I sighed and continued, 'My cousin Sally knew Melanie who was living at Kara's house in Hampstead: not the very posh bit but the bit on the other side of Swiss Cottage.' I smiled at this recollection. 'I expect it's all pretty expensive now. So my parents were happy I was going to somewhere safe. Little did they know.'

'And Gabriel? Was he living there?' She prompted me again. 'Now we're getting to the exciting bit of the story,' was written all over her face.

It wasn't easy to recall the exact details.

'Gabriel had been living there during the late sixties, but if I remember correctly he'd left by the time I arrived. Then he suddenly reappeared one day without any warning. Let me think.'

One by one I ticked them off on my fingers.

'There was Kara, of course and there was Josie. I think she was in her second year at the LSE and of course the beautiful Melanie was also living in the house.'

As I spoke, I recalled with a shudder that episode in the kitchen.

'Was she an actress?' interrupted Susie eagerly.

'No, nothing like that.' I shook my head. 'She worked in a bank, but she was so lovely, had this devastating effect on men, yet she seemed to be totally unaware of it.'

'That's it?' Susie sat back and took another mouthful of doughnut, unable to disguise her disappointment at this bland litany of events.

Said like that it sounded completely normal, with nothing in this recall of events to upset me so much. That was what was most worrying. With all that was going on in my life at the moment, I couldn't cope if memories of the accident from years ago were coming back to trouble me, were again causing me problems.

'Not quite,' I hurried on, anxious to prove there was a good reason for my strange behaviour. 'There was also George. He was very public school. Something in the city, if I remember correctly. He wasn't very bright, so whatever it was he did, I suspect a friend had pulled some strings.' Another idea came to mind. 'Though I seem to remember that his parents had been killed in a plane crash, not long before I moved in.'

Susie drained the last of her coffee while I considered this.

'That may partly explain why Josie fussed over him all the time. She was in love with him, I'm sure. And felt sorry he was all alone in the world. Cooking for him, doing his ironing: she was really smitten and he wasn't the least bit grateful. Took it all as his due, somehow. Melanie was often annoyed with her, but Josie was beyond help as far as George was concerned.'

'And ...' prompted Susie, fiddling with the last crumbs on her plate, avoiding looking at me directly.

'We all got on well together,' I added lamely. 'We'd go out to the Swiss Cottage pub together most evenings in the summer, or sometimes to the cinema, or a Sunday walk up Primrose Hill.' I shrugged, recalling the photo that had started all this. 'It's so difficult to explain if you weren't actually there.'

Susie persisted. Her voice was quiet as she said, 'And Gabriel? What about Gabriel, Alison?'

I'd left him till last, deliberately, realising everything at Kara's house in Hampstead had been perfectly normal before Gabriel came back. I took a long slow sip of my now cold coffee.

'Everything changed when Gabriel appeared.'

It was as though a curtain had come down on my memory again: something had changed when he arrived, but what?

'The details escape me, Susie; all I know is that it was all different.' I told her about the kitchen episode, lingered over the details, hoping a memory might return.

'Sounds very like selective amnesia, if you ask me,' she said stoutly, 'but maybe it will come back to you, like that episode in the kitchen. Possibly there's something that's too painful to recall at the moment.'

I could only nod dumbly, grateful for her understanding. If I couldn't remember, did that mean there was something terrible I'd suppressed and, even worse, wouldn't be able to cope if I did? That thought terrified me.

She visibly brightened and pushed her plate to the side, wetting her finger to pick up the last of the sugary crumbs.

'Have you thought of trying to find of a copy of Gabriel's death certificate? That would settle it all for you.'

'What if he isn't dead? What if it was all some horrible mistake? Where would I look then?'

'You could try the Salvation Army for a start.'

This wasn't helpful.

'I don't see Gabriel being the sort of person to turn to religion somehow.'

Susie laughed loudly at this reply, and the two elderly women at the next table craned over, curious to know what was causing such hilarity.

She continued to laugh, albeit more quietly, as I motioned her to stop, reluctant to provide entertainment for the other customers.

'You've got it all wrong, Alison. The Salvation Army has a branch that helps in tracing missing friends and relatives.'

This was too simple: if Gabriel was still alive, he'd have covered his tracks well, but all I said was, 'I don't think I could be in any way classified as a friend, never mind a relative.' A moment later, sensing her disappointment at my lack of enthusiasm for her suggestion, I added, 'Don't worry, Susie, it's not that important.'

A hurt look crossed her face.

'I thought you wanted my opinion? And I think you need some help. You've been so strung out and touchy lately. You can't go on like this.'

The next few minutes were spent convincing her she had indeed been helpful, even by listening to me. This wasn't entirely true and I suspect she knew it. We've been friends for too long to be able to dissemble.

After making me promise to let her know if I remembered anything else, or felt the need to talk, she said, 'Why don't you try to put it all out of your mind and relax and enjoy Christmas. You and Simon can go down to London at half term and ferret around there. See if it's still an issue when you're back to where it all happened, so to speak. Satisfy yourself by checking the original records.'

When there was no reaction, she went on, 'If the records say Gabriel is dead then accept it. It was all a long time ago and imagination can make us believe all sorts of things. It may be something quite different that's making you think you saw him. It'll come back to you eventually. It may not be anything to do with this Gabriel.'

Reluctantly I agreed. I'd hoped Susie would convince me it was all down to stress or my imagination, to go away and forget about it altogether, but she didn't, leaving me with that awful feeling there might be something to this sighting after all. Truth was, I didn't want to find out the answer about Gabriel, didn't want to remember. All I needed now was for the whole episode to go away.

It was only later that night, lying awake in the dark, listening to Simon's heavy breathing, I suddenly realised what it was that had been nagging away at me since my conversation with Susie. Even if the records did show that Gabriel had died, how could I be sure that the body they had dragged from Hampstead Pond had been his?

And if it wasn't his body, whose body was it?

EIGHT

There were so many strange things going on in that house in Hampstead immediately before Gabriel died. In spite of struggling to find some fragment of memory to make sense of it all, nothing helped. Kara had identified him, but she too was dead.

In the darkness, I went over and over the same ground, but there was no blinding flash of inspiration, no recollection to provide an answer.

The illuminated dial of the bedside clock showed three a.m. At this rate I'd be fit for nothing in the morning and I had a particularly troublesome second year class to deal with first thing.

Lying there in the dark I made the decision to take Susie's advice. We could visit Maura at half term and if the records did indeed show Gabriel Santos had died, I'd forget all about it. After all, I'd caught only the merest glimpse of that man on the train: some association had triggered my subconscious. It was a mistake.

Wasn't there such a thing as false memory syndrome? In the muddled memories that had returned after the accident I was confusing events and might even be remembering something I'd been told rather than actually experienced.

Reassured a little, almost convinced by this line or reasoning, I settled down to sleep, but it was some time before I drifted off and in that half state between waking and sleeping imagined myself drowning, while above me stood Gabriel, ignoring my pleas for help.

After what seemed like only a few moments the shrill sound of the alarm clock startled me into wakefulness. Beside me, Simon stirred then lapsed back into sleep. For a few moments I lay immobile, trying to still my racing heart.

Making a determined effort not to disturb him, I eased myself out of bed, but to no avail. He awoke, yawning as he propped himself up on the pillow.

'More bad dreams, Alison? Tell me, for goodness sake.'

Was this genuine concern for my welfare? Whatever his reason, there was no point in alarming him.

'I'm always dreaming, Simon, you know that, but my nightmares disappear with the daylight,' I said, going over to look out of the window so he couldn't see the expression on my face.

'Well, if you do have memories surfacing, even in your dreams, make sure to tell me.' He frowned. 'I want to help you.'

Up and dressed, having drunk two cups of coffee, I felt much better about the decision to travel to London and put all thoughts of Gabriel out of my mind, determined to enjoy Christmas.

In the end it wasn't that simple. It was as if everything and everyone was conspiring to increase my feeling of unease. Strangely enough, it was Simon who was indirectly the cause of my next trauma, even though at the time it seemed such a good idea, designed to give me a boost pre-Christmas.

'Alison, do you fancy a trip to the opera at the Theatre Royal?'

He was grinning like a Cheshire cat as he spoke, trying hard to contain his glee.

Not wanting to spoil the surprise, 'Well...' I said, 'although I like music, opera isn't really my favourite.' Visions of having to sit through a very highbrow performance or a complicated plot, something I was in no mood for in my present state, came to mind. On the other hand, better to be tactful.

'Don't worry,' he went on hurriedly, pre-empting any further comments. 'It's *Carmen* I'm suggesting. I'm sure you'd enjoy that. You've been so down recently it would do you good to get out. Pep you up for Christmas.' He looked at me anxiously, trying to anticipate my response.

Thank goodness this was what he'd chosen. *Carmen* was a favourite of mine. Then, 'Isn't that a bit extravagant before Christmas?'

'Oh, they were very cheap,' he grinned, finally giving away his secret. 'In fact, they were free. From Jimmy McLeod. You remember him? He teaches Drama at the college. He bought them a while back and now he's found out it's the same night as his daughter's school Christmas concert. I gather the young Miss McLeod has a starring role, so there's no way he can miss it for a trip to the opera.'

The Theatre Royal's a great place: very atmospheric with all that Victorian gilt and plush and any occasion there is a real treat. This was an opportunity too good to refuse.

Simon grinned triumphantly. 'That's agreed then. Tuesday night we're off to *Carmen*.'

We'd been so busy at school there'd been no opportunity to follow up on my discussions with Susie. Just as well. Without meaning to, I'd avoided her. Exams to mark, not to mention helping organise the upper school disco, kept my mind fully occupied.

About a week after the video episode I bumped into Susie in the corridor as we were both hurrying to our respective classes. She caught me by the arm, forcing me to stop for a few moments.

'I've been thinking about that problem of yours, Alison,' she said, swinging round and cornering me so there was no means of escape. 'I've put an article I found in *Psychology Unlimited* in your tray. I think you should read it: it might explain a lot.'

Before I could ask exactly what she meant, one of the first year girls appeared round the corner sobbing hysterically, and Susie disappeared off with her in a flurry of soothing words, leaving me gazing after her.

I was already late for my class, and had no option but to contain my curiosity, but was so distracted even my fourth year class noticed it and several times I caught one of them nudging the person beside him and tittering. It was obvious my mind wasn't entirely on the lesson.

Listening to their answers to the homework interpretation set the week before, my mind kept wandering and I was only brought back to the present by a sudden awareness that a complete silence had descended.

William Smith, who'd been attempting to give his answer to one of the more difficult questions, was speaking to me. 'I said, Miss,' he repeated loudly, 'I wasn't sure if that was quite correct.'

There were a few muffled sniggers. Everyone else was looking at me expectantly, willing something exciting to happen to liven up the lesson and I made a gallant effort to bluff my way out.

'If you could repeat it once more so that the rest of the class can hear,' I replied, trying to compose myself. There was more suppressed laughter which I did my best to quell with a glare, but was as eager as they were for the lesson to end.

A few minutes before the bell rang for lunchtime I dismissed them, watching them scurry off with some relief.

After tidying up and gathering my papers together, I went straight to the staffroom to pick up the article Susie had left in my tray. She'd carefully positioned it on top of the usual memos and alterations to timetables that appear with alarming frequency.

In need of somewhere to think, somewhere quiet before anyone could engage me in conversation, I hurried along to the library where there would be the opportunity to read it undisturbed. At a corner desk, well away from prying eyes, I sat down and opened the article Susie had copied for me.

At first I was puzzled, as it seemed to be all about some woman whose mother had died after a long illness and mine was very much alive, but I persevered and then light began to dawn.

Apparently (or so the learned author claimed through rigorous research) this woman began to suffer post bereavement hallucinations where she imagined she saw and heard her mother in the most unusual locations and at the oddest times. Well, it was true I'd seen Gabriel, but I hadn't heard him. And I'd only seen him once, if you didn't count the video. Even so, the article was pretty alarming as some of the causes of such hallucinations (according to the respected author) could be stress or worse - a brain tumour or mental illness.

I gathered my jacket more tightly around me. Was I seriously ill without knowing it? Was whatever was happening to me a legacy of that car crash, some effect only now surfacing after all these years?

Carefully I examined my face in the pocket mirror pulled from my handbag. No, I looked no paler than before and the only noticeable thing, which depressed me even more, was that my roots needed retouching.

Or had I suffered some new trauma? There was nothing that might have set off that first sighting of Gabriel, but those memories had been suppressed for so long I might have genuinely forgotten them.

Everyone had told me how well I'd recovered from the accident. What if they were wrong? Or worse still, lying?

About to fold up the article, dismiss it as not relevant, I paused. If I had seen someone on the train who looked like Gabriel, what would happen next?

That made me more afraid than ever. Now these reminders of the past had somehow been triggered off, I could hardly bear the idea I might keep seeing his apparition. Recollections of the episode in Fraser's department store flooded back and I could feel my cheeks burning at the thought.

I wrote quickly on the copy, 'Many thanks, Susie, most interesting,' and left the library hurriedly, hoping to slip it into Susie's tray before she made it to the staffroom.

I then spent the rest of the day trying to avoid her and left as fast as possible at the end of the school day by the back exit, in no mood for my usual collapse in the staffroom with a cup of tea.

Echoes of the past were returning unbidden and I lived in dread of what might happen next.

NINE

On Tuesday night, as we were getting ready to go to the Theatre Royal, Maura phoned. I was about to step into the shower and Simon was about to start fretting in case we'd be late. This time it wasn't my fault: a staff meeting at school had overrun, so time was tight.

'I'll be quick, Mum, since you're in a rush. I'm phoning to let you know I've arranged some time off over Christmas - and New Year as well.'

'How did you manage that?' I asked in some astonishment, understanding how difficult Maura finds it to book any holiday time, working as she does for a small advertising agency whose financial affairs seem to be in a permanent state of crisis.

She chuckled, 'Oh, I played the Scottish card. We're closing for Christmas after last year's fiasco when we seemed to be the only people in London still working. And I convinced Tom that you and dad would be heartbroken if I didn't manage to spend at least one New Year with my family.'

It was much more likely she'd be spending New Year at the street party in Edinburgh where some of her friends have a flat, or bringing it in with Deborah's Glasgow friends, but all I said was, 'You must have an understanding boss, Maura.'

'Yes, he is rather sweet,' she replied without the slightest trace of irony.

She's pretty much like her father in this way. Not only does she look like him, she has his charm. "Sweet" isn't the word I'd use to describe the six foot four rugby player who is Maura's boss.

'Great,' I said. 'We'll look forward to seeing a lot more of you this holiday.' To date her visits have been confined to weekend flying visits.

Simon came downstairs, pointing at his watch and frowning. 'Who's that on the phone?' he hissed.

I put my hand over the mouthpiece. 'It's Maura. Why don't you speak to her while I have a quick shower?'

As I was about to pass the receiver to him, she said, 'Oh, by the way, Mum, did you read that newspaper article I sent you? The one about that guy who drowned? I'm looking forward to you telling me all about it when I come home.'

My heart was thudding so hard I was sure it could be heard all the way to London. Simon stared at me, as though he could read my mind, but that idea was nonsense and I managed to say in a very shaky voice, 'No, I haven't had time to read it yet Maura. We can talk about it when I see you. Goodbye, dear, here's Dad.' I handed the receiver to him and fled upstairs.

It was all so stupid, but it seemed the harder I tried to put the sighting of Gabriel out of my mind the more everyone else conspired to prompt my memory.

Why couldn't I have said to her, 'Of course I remember it all, Maura, but it was all a long time ago and you know what newspapers make of the slightest story.' Thankfully there was no time for further deliberation: we were now running very late and I still had to find something suitable to wear.

'What was that all about? What did Maura say to upset you?' Simon broke into my thoughts as he came into the bedroom.

'Nothing important,' I replied with false gaiety and tried to distract him. 'Do you think I should wear my grey trouser suit or my new green wool dress?' I held both up for his inspection, carefully avoiding his direct gaze.

He didn't answer my question, but persisted. 'It looked to me as if you'd had bad news.'

'Not at all,' I said as lightly as possible before hurrying on, 'I'll wear my grey trouser suit, in case there's any walking involved.' And, I added silently, in case we go for a meal afterwards. My grey trousers have an elastic waistband, where as the green wool dress was bought on one of those days where I was convinced I'd be disciplined enough to lose a few pounds before Christmas.

'Did Maura tell you she's planning to come home for Christmas and New Year?' I asked. This tack of changing the subject finally worked.

'Well, as long as none of the others descends for long. I don't fancy having to move all the stuff out of my study like last year.'

How was I going to tell him that not only were all three children planning to be with us for the whole festive period, but my mother had suddenly announced she thought she'd stay on with us for a while?

There was no more time to discuss Christmas plans: we had to hurry if we wanted to arrive at the theatre in time, given the unpredictability of the traffic.

Our seats were right at the front of the Dress Circle with a full view of the stage. Jimmy McLeod hadn't stinted on cost and I only hoped he would be enjoying his daughter's concert as much as we were going to enjoy the opera, though I doubted it.

'This is a great seat,' I whispered to Simon as the orchestra tuned up to strike up the overture, feeling my spirits lift as we prepared for the intrigues of *Carmen*.

Simon studied the programme in the dimmed lighting while I gazed round the theatre, pleased to see a full house, and then leaned forward eagerly over the balustrade.

'What on earth are you doing, Alison?' hissed Simon.

'I'm trying to see if there's anyone I recognise here tonight. You know what it's like: you can't go anywhere in Glasgow without bumping into someone you know.'

He merely shook his head and went back to scanning the programme.

My survey of the stalls having failed to come up with anyone familiar, I glanced idly over to the Boxes, though it wasn't likely any of my friends would be there.

Then I froze. There he was, in the Box right next to the stage. My view couldn't have been clearer but although I tried to speak, no more than a croak came out. I tugged at Simon's sleeve.

He lifted his eyes from the programme. 'What is it Alison? Why are you tugging my jacket, for goodness sake?'

'Over there, in the Box near the stage,' I finally managed to squeak, my heart thudding fit to burst.

Annoyed, but not wanting to cause a fuss, he followed my pointing finger as I said, 'It's Gabriel Santos.'

TEN

'Are you sure?' This time Simon sounded very concerned.

A second inspection of the Box showed that Gabriel, if indeed it was Gabriel, had turned to speak to the woman sitting beside him and only the back of his head was visible, not enough in this light to confirm my suspicions.

Simon muttered, 'How can you be so certain, Alison, with his back to us and at this distance?'

He grabbed my hand, probably to make sure I wouldn't do anything silly. Now sounding cross, probably imagining his evening was about to be spoiled by my hysteria, he said, 'Calm down and enjoy the opera. It's impossible to make out anything in this gloom.'

Tempted to say that the lighting had nothing to do with it, I suddenly remembered my earlier "sightings", particularly the very embarrassing one in Fraser's department store, and kept silent. Was Gabriel here deliberately to upset me? What nonsense. There was no way he could know we'd have tickets for this evening. I was becoming obsessed with this. Taking a deep breath, I grabbed the programme from Simon and began to study it intently.

Then, as the orchestra came in, ready to tune up, Simon did the oddest thing. He abruptly left his seat saying, 'Won't be a minute. I forgot to order drinks for the interval.'

Too astonished to protest, I could only watch as he bounded up the stairs towards the bar and when he returned a few minutes later he seemed almost jovial as he flopped into his seat with a, 'Sorry about that.'

By now the lights had dimmed, the orchestra struck up with a flourish and the woman behind us tutted loudly.

Curious to know why he'd suddenly decided to pre-order drinks, I started to speak, but he put his finger to his lips and shook his head warningly.

In spite of all my efforts to concentrate, my eyes kept being drawn to where Gabriel sat, willing him to turn round again, give me a better view.

As the first Act began it seemed my wish was about to be granted as the man in the Box swung back and for a moment appeared to be gazing directly at me, which was nonsense of course. Even so, I shrank down in my seat, trying my best to hide behind Simon.

'Will you kindly stop this,' Simon muttered, pushing me away. 'You're beginning to imagine this Gabriel Santos everywhere.'

Not quite everywhere, I thought, but enough to alarm me, remembering the article Susie had given me.

'Anyway,' he went on in a low voice, conscious of the glares of anger from the surrounding theatregoers, 'if you're so certain it's Gabriel, why don't you confront him? Go round to see him or check the bar during the interval when we go for a drink. I'll be there with you.'

A wave of relief swept over me. It was as simple as that. There was no reason to be afraid of Gabriel. Far better to go up and speak to him, as if he was no more than any acquaintance from my past. And if Simon was willing to come with me, I'd feel a whole lot braver. But what would I say? 'Hi, Gabriel, I see you're not dead after all?'

This was so ridiculous I had to ferret in my handbag for a handkerchief to stifle my laughter, eventually managing with some effort to control myself, but it was now impossible to concentrate on what was happening on the stage.

The first Act played out, but my attention kept wandering, and I spent most of the time rehearsing scenarios about what to say when we finally confronted Gabriel. My first action would be to introduce him to Simon, whose presence would be very reassuring.

Was it Gabriel? What if this was another mistake? One minute I was sure he'd been the person on that train, the next that it was only someone who looked like him.

Beside me, Simon shifted restlessly in his seat and I made a determined effort to engage with the events on stage, to avoid looking in the direction of the Box. It all seemed to take forever and when at last the curtain came down for the interval on Carmen, Jose and Zuniga, I'm sure my applause was the loudest in the theatre.

Slowly, very slowly, as the lights went up, I took a deep breath and gazed over towards the Box. Perhaps now I'd be able to see for sure, determine if it was indeed Gabriel before involving Simon in yet another wild goose chase. To my horror, the Box was empty and it was all I could do to stifle a scream.

Simon followed my gaze and immediately realised what was wrong. He quickly grabbed my hand.

'Most likely they've gone out early to get to the bar before the crush. It's easier to do that from a Box than from the middle of a row. Or maybe they're not too keen on the performance.'

'Let's see if we can find them, please,' I pleaded

We stood up and edged our way through the chattering, slow moving crowd thronging the stairway, much to the annoyance of several elderly ladies who appeared to be on a pre-Christmas outing.

'Some people can't wait to get to the bar,' one of them remarked frostily.

Ignoring this comment I pushed on, holding Simon so tightly by the hand he'd no option but to follow me as I nudged those at the top of the stairs to move. Unfortunately for me, everyone was in relaxed good humour and in no hurry: I was the only one who'd something urgent to do.

As I'd absolutely no idea what to say when face to face with Gabriel, all my attention was focused on reaching the bar, hoping inspiration would come to me, but in the crush of noisy theatregoers there was no sign of him anywhere in the bar.

I leaned for support against the ledge fixed at waist level round the room, and a sense of bitter disappointment flooded through me as I bit my lip in a bid to stop my tears of frustration.

Then suddenly Simon was beside me repeating, 'What do you want to drink, Alison?'

Why was he asking me this if he'd ordered the drinks in advance? I was about to challenge him, but some sixth sense held me back and I stared at him, trying to decide what he was up to. He looked back at me, giving nothing away.

'A glass of white wine would do nicely,' I said, then called as he headed for the bar, 'Make it a large one.'

When Simon came back, brandishing the drinks aloft over the heads of the crowd, I took the glass from him and gulped it down the wine as though it was water.

'Hey, steady on,' he said, frowning at my speed of dispatch, 'I don't want you falling asleep during the rest of the performance.'

The adrenaline was still pumping through my veins and this remark had the effect of making me furious. 'Yes, I will have another one thank you, Simon,' I said firmly and rather than make a fuss in such a public place, he went off to fetch my order.

'Drink this one slowly,' he said as he handed it to me a few moments later.

It all worked against me, of course, because the interval is scarcely enough time for one drink, never mind two, and I was more than a little unsteady on my feet as I followed Simon back to the Dress circle, bitterly disappointed at this turn of events.

Simon, on the other hand, seemed almost cheerful, making me suspect he was more than a little relieved. He'd probably not been the least convinced that it had been Gabriel and the disappearance of the man in the Box had saved him from a potentially embarrassing situation.

Halfway up the stairs I suddenly stopped. What if they'd gone to one of the other bars? How stupid. Why hadn't I considered that possibility sooner? Instead of wasting time drinking two large glasses of wine, which I now bitterly regretted as they were sloshing around in my stomach, making me feel decidedly queasy, I should've gone round all the other bars in the theatre.

There was no way to persuade Simon to start this search with me now, as the performance was about to begin again.

Suddenly inspired, I put my hand on his arm saying, 'Won't be a minute. Have to go to the Ladies. See you upstairs,' and rushed off before he could reply. It wasn't original, but it was the best I could come up with in the circumstances.

As fast as the crowds returning to their seats permitted, I edged my way to the next bar up, ignoring the summons of the warning bell. Only a minute of the interval remained and there was still no sign of Gabriel and his companion. Totally frustrated, I ran to the bar on the half landing. Empty! Even the most hardened drinkers had disappeared back into the auditorium.

There was nothing else for it. I had to go to the Box and find out for myself if they'd returned, and I ignored the sound of the final warning bell as I reached the entrance.

Now beyond any rational action, I opened the door no more than a crack. It was my intention to have a quick look and retreat with a "sorry" before being spotted, but at least I'd know one way or the other if it really was Gabriel.

No longer feeling afraid, believing this was my sanity at stake, I pushed the door open as quietly and as slowly as possible, each tiny squeak sounding like a peal of thunder. For this to work, I had to have time to have a reasonably good look at Gabriel's face, but not stay long enough for him to recognise me, so I put my free hand up over my face and tried to peer through my fingers.

I needn't have worried. The Box was completely deserted except for a discarded programme lying on one of the seats. Although there was no one to notice, I closed the door carefully and stood there for a few moments trying to control my trembling, drained by disappointment.

Over on the stage Carmen and her friends Frasquita and Mercedes were engaged in reading Tarot cards. Standing outside the Box, unable to move, I felt faint: a combination of too much wine and too much excitement. Simon would be furious with me, but it was too late to return to my seat. Attempting to squeeze in now that the performance had started again wouldn't exactly make me popular with the theatregoers in our row. Whatever had happened, Gabriel or his double was no longer in the theatre.

Sick with nerves, upset, and in need of fresh air, I forced myself to move, made my way down through the silent corridors to push open the main door into the foyer.

'The performance has started again, madam,' said a helpful usher, 'but you can sneak in and wait at the back if you want.'

This wasn't what I wanted at all. I needed to go outside in the hope the cool night air might revive me. I could always do as the usher suggested later - watch the rest of the opera from the back of the stalls. If I could face it.

Out on the street I stood inhaling deeply, watching my breath make little wraiths of mist in the cold evening air, waiting for my heart to stop pounding.

As well as feeling sick, baffled and strangely let down, I was feeling wretchedly guilty. Guilty about using Mr McLeod's very expensive tickets, guilty about spoiling Simon's evening and guilty about imposing my wild imaginings on all and sundry, but gradually, as I stood there, my heart slowed to a more normal pace.

I'd almost decided to go back in to the theatre, hoping be able to say something sensible about the performance should I ever come face to face with Mr McLeod, but as I turned away, a taxi drew up further along the street and stopped directly outside the Café Royal on the corner.

Two people came hurrying through the heavy wooden entrance doors and scurried into the cab. As it made its way slowly past me into the stream of traffic the lights went to red and it paused for a moment right beside me. Directly in my line of vision, in the back seat, was Gabriel.

He gazed across at me and for one moment those glittering eyes, amber and still as a cat's, held my horrified gaze. A lazy smile crossed his face and slowly, slowly he lifted his hand to wave. A quick look round confirmed there was no one else in sight: there could be no doubt he was waving at me.

Standing motionless at the front of the theatre, watching in fascinated horror as the taxi gathered speed and disappeared round the corner into Cowcaddens Road, I'd no idea what to think.

Had Gabriel seen me in the theatre? He must have realised exactly who I was, judging by the way he'd drawn attention to himself.

Of course, there was no other explanation. Gabriel had not only seen me, but had gone out of his way to make sure he was visible. He was trying to frighten me.

What was worse, I recognised the woman sitting beside him in the taxi. It was Melanie.

ELEVEN

It's not a good idea to keep a diary: you're tempted to be too frank, to entrust to it all kinds of secrets - a disaster if it falls into the hands of the wrong person. I didn't remember keeping a diary all those years ago in Hampstead, but was soon to find out this was part of the jigsaw of my past.

The holidays were close upon us and I was slowly learning to live with this permanent feeling of unease about whether Gabriel was alive or dead. During the weeks of Christmas festivities, forcing myself to be hearty and cheerful, I'd tried to put it all to the back of my mind, but every memory of Gabriel's face looking out from that taxi made my blood run cold. And I couldn't think of any reason why Melanie would be with him.

Christmas and New Year passed in a flurry of activity. All three children came home for at least some of the time and with my mother also staying over, there were few opportunities to think constructively about the problem. Just as well. There's nothing like frantic activity to stop you fretting.

Maura attempted several times to ask me about the article in the *Ham and High* but I carefully sidestepped any discussion. Then, on top of everything else, we had to take poor Motley to the vet.

'There's absolutely nothing wrong with him,' insisted Simon. 'It's all those treats and spoiling he's getting.' He glared pointedly at my mother. 'He's suffering from some form of over-indulgence.'

She took absolutely no notice, went on reading the newspaper in that way she has of blanking everything and everyone out.

'I thought as the children grew up Christmas would mean less work, not more,' he said plaintively and I had to turn away to suppress a smile.

Any opportunity to worry was lost in the usual mayhem once the children were back home, bringing assorted friends who dropped in and out, so that keeping the fridge stocked proved a challenge. They stayed out late, often returning at two and three in the morning and lying in bed till midday the next day.

'I'm not sure we can cope with this any more,' I said to Simon one morning in sheer exhaustion. Yet again, we'd only managed finally to fall asleep in the early hours.

Christmas Eve found us in the living room trying to finish wrapping the presents. I was kneeling on the floor, struggling to extricate myself from the sellotape which had somehow contrived to wind itself round my fingers instead of round the parcel, while Simon was wrestling with the Christmas tree. The last one left at the garden centre which hadn't quite lost all its needles, it was no beauty, but once we'd covered it with plenty of tinsel, decorations and fairy lights it would pass muster.

'Are you sure this is straight?' he said yet again, struggling with the tree holder.

I looked up from trying to find the start of the sellotape. 'Absolutely fine,' I said, but he wasn't convinced. To distract him I went on, 'When are you going to collect Gerry?' Simon's only brother is a brilliant mathematician but a terrible timekeeper.

He looked at his watch. 'I said I'd be there about four o'clock, so it should be fine if I leave in about half an hour or so.'

'Well, remember the traffic might be busy.'

'Don't worry, Alison. I'll collect him as soon as we've finished putting up this tree.'

'You will be nice to him, won't you, Simon?' I looked at him doubtfully.

By this time he had succeeded in setting up the tree to his satisfaction and was only half listening. He said vaguely, 'Of course, of course,' looking at me as if he didn't understand. 'I'm always nice to Gerry,' he said.

'No, you're not,' I retorted. 'Look at that great fall out you had last Christmas over which programme we should watch on Christmas night.'

He groaned, 'Did you have to remind me about that? Anyway, with a bit of luck I'll get some of the items on my Christmas list this year and can occupy myself nicely.'

This was a sore point. It was most unfair of him to remind me that last year we'd lost his carefully prepared list of suggestions. As a result we'd all had to make a wild stab at what he might want, none too successfully. Better to say no more on the subject.

'Now, Alison,' said Simon, standing back and regarding his handiwork with some satisfaction, 'that's all the fairy lights on. What about the decorations?'

Oh dear. The decorations were still in the box at the back of the attic where they'd been abandoned last year before my rush back to school.

'They're still in the attic, aren't they?' he said, as though reading my mind. Fortunately he'd regained his good humour. He looked at my stricken face. 'I'll go and dig them out them if you put the kettle on for some tea.'

Hopefully they were somewhere accessible and he wouldn't put his foot through the ceiling as he walked about on that part of the attic he hadn't got round to flooring.

Fifteen minutes later and there was still no sign of him. Out of deference to the Christmas spirit, I'd unearthed our only real teapot instead of my usual method of throwing a teabag into each cup. Concerned the tea was stewing, I left the kitchen and went upstairs to the attic hatch, shouting 'Have you found them yet?'

There was a muffled reply, so I gingerly climbed the first few steps of the ladder and poked my head through the opening.

Simon was crouched in the corner. By the poor light of the one central bulb which scarcely penetrated the gloom he was engrossed in reading something, and gave a start when he saw me.

'What on earth are you up to?' I said crossly. 'This tea will be cold if you don't come down now.'

He got up suddenly, banging his head on the rafters. 'Ouch! Won't be a moment.' He lifted the box of decorations and edged his way over to the attic hatch.

'What were you doing up there?'

He set the box down on the table. 'Nothing, really. Some of the decorations had escaped the box and as I gathered them up, I was distracted rooting through all the bits and pieces we stored there. You know what it's like. Now,' very briskly, 'where's that tea?'

Later, with the tree suitably adorned and the wrapped presents in a cheerful pile beneath its glittering branches, I said, 'I really think you should collect Gerry.

'I'm leaving now,' he said, and went into the hall. As he was putting his coat on the phone rang. 'I'll get it,' he shouted through to me.

I'd no intention of listening in to his conversation, but with all that had been going on couldn't help myself, though all I could catch was a few muttered words of his side of the conversation.

'Promises again…worse than before…can't see a solution.' His tone sounded angry, aggrieved.

When he came back into the room I asked, pretending to be scrutinising the labels on the parcels, 'Who was that?'

He hesitated for a few moments, avoiding looking at me. 'Work,' was the abrupt reply. 'I'll go and collect Gerry.' With that he was gone, slamming the door behind him.

There was no time to fret about the phone call and as soon as the sound of his car driving away died in the distance, I ran back upstairs.

I've a bit of a phobia about going up to the attic, never feeling the ladder is quite secure enough, but this time my determination drove me on. What had Simon found up here? Because I was certain he'd found something he didn't want me to see.

Once up in the dusty recesses, I crawled slowly and carefully on my hands and knees over to the corner where Simon had been, but in spite of exploring the various boxes, there was absolutely nothing that might have captured his attention.

Defeated, I sat down on one of the beams near the spot where I'd seen him, gazing all round, trying to guess where whatever he'd found might be, where he would have hidden it quickly.

I closed my eyes and felt at the back of the wooden struts, stuck my hand down in the space between the rafters and the eaves and after a few minutes my fingers touched something thick. Was this what he'd been reading?

Moving carefully to keep my balance, I eased it out. To my surprise it was an old blue exercise book, the kind schools used to use, complete with mathematical tables about important measures like bushels and pecks. I blew off the dust and opened it with some trepidation. Surely it couldn't be? It was.

There in my own handwriting on the first page inside it said *Alison Fraser: Diary*. Why was it here in the attic? I was sure this had been thrown out with most of the rest of the stuff from that time. Had Simon rescued it and hidden it?

I couldn't leave now and tried to make myself as comfortable as possible on one of the joists, wriggling about till I judged my position relatively safe, before slowly opening the first page and starting to flick through it more and more quickly, beginning to feel almost faint as those names from the past leapt off the pages: Kara, George, Melanie, Josie.

Was there anything in this diary that might be of use? Why had Simon not let me know it was still here? It was exactly the sort of thing that might have allowed me come to terms with what was happening, helped me fill in the missing bits of my memory.

It was a very personal record, almost self obsessed. No mention here of the big events of the day: the Vietnam war, Idi Amin seizing power in Uganda, the successful Apollo 14 and 15 missions, the end of the Postal strike in Britain(a major inconvenience), not even a word about the death of Jim Morrison of The Doors. None of these merited a passing reference. An indication of how involved I was in the minutiae of my social life in those days.

The faint chiming of the hall clock brought me back to the present. Simon would be home soon and I had to make a decision: whether to take the diary downstairs to read it through now, or put it back where I'd found it.

Cramp started in my legs and I adjusted my position, almost falling off the wooden beam in the process. There was no time to go through the rest of this book at this moment and if it had been hidden in the attic for all this time, it would surely be safe here for a little longer.

I couldn't explain why I didn't want Simon to know I'd found it but, confused about what to do, made the decision to replace it exactly where it had been hidden, planning to come up again and retrieve it for a safe hiding place as soon as an opportunity arose.

Once I'd had time to read through it carefully, surely this diary would help me recall the details of those memories that were so upsetting me. Would help me remember enough about Gabriel to lay his ghost forever.

TWELVE

The diary had disappeared.

Later in the evening, after dinner, when everyone was slumped in front of the television watching some very frantic game show, I'd managed to sneak back to the attic. The noise of the television, raised to an ear-shattering volume at my mother's request, drowned out the creak of the ladder coming down and my hasty scramble up. It was no use. In spite of an increasingly frantic search where I thought I'd left it, and then into the furthest corners, increasingly careless of the risk of falling, I eventually had to admit defeat. Wherever the diary was, it wasn't here. How stupid not to move it earlier, hide it somewhere more accessible.

I edged my way over to the beam nearest the trapdoor and sat down carefully, trying to decide if I should start the search again. There was no point, the diary was gone, and I crept down to join the others. No one seemed to have missed me and under cover of the television programme there was at least time to think, but no solution to the problem of the missing diary came to mind, there was no sudden revelation about what might have happened to it.

Then, as I stood at the sink very early on Christmas morning, peeling potatoes for lunch, I'd a sudden insight. If Simon had been the only other person in the attic, he must have removed the diary while I was busy making dinner the previous evening.

I considered whether there was time to sneak away and try to find out what he'd done with it, where he'd stashed it. It must still be in the house somewhere: he surely wouldn't have risked binning it.

Too late. Another missed opportunity as the early birds straggled down for breakfast, though there was still no sign of life from Deborah and Alastair.

When those of us who'd ventured out for the Christmas service returned, Alastair and Deborah had not only surfaced but the coffee pot was bubbling merrily on the stove and by the time we'd finished a leisurely coffee we all pitched in to make sure lunch was ready more or less on time.

'Time for a drink?' said Simon hopefully as he joined me in the kitchen.

'Great idea.'

Usually I'd veto drinks until the first course was on the table. There have been one or two unfortunate experiences over the years.

When Simon went off find out what everyone wanted to drink, and with the meal now well under control, I said loudly, 'I'm going for a quick bath.' Why I bothered with this ploy, I'm not sure. Everyone was too busy to pay much attention.

I slipped from the room, reckoning I'd a reasonable time for my search and, once in the bathroom, turned on the taps to a slow trickle and set the radio to maximum volume.

Simon must have put the diary somewhere within easy reach, given the very limited time he'd had to hide it.

The first place to look was his study and I crept along the hallway, glancing round to check there was no one about before opening the door cautiously. Once inside I stopped and gazed around in dismay. The diary could be anywhere in this room: in his desk, hidden among the piles of papers, stowed in the filing cabinet. He might even have found a good place among the many books ranged higgedly-piggedly on the shelves.

Conscious of time passing, I flicked through the papers on his desk more and more quickly, opened desk drawers as quietly as possible, trying not to disturb anything. I didn't want him to know what I was up to, though what reason was there not to ask him about the diary, tell him I'd found it in the attic? Because I didn't want him to know of my suspicions, that was why. He'd only give me some good reason, some plausible explanation about not wanting to upset me. Trouble was, I wouldn't have believed him.

The hall clock chimed the hour: time was running out. This was madness: the diary could be anywhere, might no longer be in the house. And there was no excuse I could think of to go rummaging round in the shed at the bottom of the garden at this time on Christmas Day.

A great wave of frustration hit me and I felt like crying. What was happening to me? If Simon didn't want me to know about the diary in case it would affect me, he might well have disposed of it. No matter what the reason, I couldn't delay any longer and left the room on tiptoe, looking back to make sure everything was in its original place.

No time now even for a shower and I emptied the bath before going into the bedroom. In my rush to get ready, I didn't hear the loud knock over the noise of the hairdryer and was startled when my mother put her head round the door.

'Hi, Mum, any problems?'

'No, no, dear, none at all. Everyone seems very happy. Simon is fetching us all another drink.'

Panic visions of the turkey being burned to a cinder or the oven breaking down subsided. Oops, I thought, I'd better be quick.

My mother went on, 'I'm so forgetful nowadays and I wanted to make sure I remembered to give you this.'

She handed me a packet of photographs, very old photographs judging by the torn cover with the imprint of *Gratispool.*

She said, 'I started to do a bit of clearing in that old chest of drawers in the spare room last week and came across these. You sent them to Dad and me when you were living in London so you might like to have them back.'

Taken by surprise, I didn't think to remonstrate with her about tackling heavy cleaning at her age and besides, a tight knot was gathering in the pit of my stomach as she held them out.

'Go on, dear, take them, I'm sure they'll bring back some pleasant memories.'

I grasped the packet with trembling hands and slowly pulled up the covering flap. 'What photos are they?' My voice trembled in spite of my attempts to appear calm.

'Oh, some photos of that place you stayed in when you first went down.' She waved her hand airily, 'You remember: that place you stayed in with Kara.'

Unable to think of a reply, I stared at her, reluctant to look at the photos.

She paused at the door as she went out of the room. 'Anyway, dear, there's no need to start going through them all now. They'll be nice to sit down with some night and remember those times. And,' she gave a girlish giggle, 'I'm sure Simon will have poured my next drink by now. A little pre-prandial he called it.'

How many drinks had Simon been dispensing? And if anyone could do with a strong drink at that moment it was me.

As soon as she left, I turned the packet over several times before fully opening it, realising there was no possibility of putting it aside till later, even if lunch was ruined. Look what had happened when I'd decided to leave the diary in the attic.

The packet held a pile of photos, some of them so old they were fused together and I carefully prised them apart. I'd almost forgotten these, sent regularly with my letters to my mother to convince her that where I was living was eminently respectable and that life in London wasn't as dangerous as she feared.

Slowly, one by one, I went through them: a record of those early days in Kara's house. There was the room I'd shared with Melanie when I'd first arrived, that familiar cluttered kitchen where we'd spent so much time together, Josie caught unaware, smiling broadly. I'd no idea how attractive she could be when she smiled. So often she looked worried, unkempt.

Realising I'd have to join the others very soon, I began to scan them rapidly, photo after photo. George, Melanie, Josie: they were all there. The past stared back at me. Melanie and I posing at the window of her room in our brand new miniskirts bought at great expense in Carnaby Street, Melanie and Josie fooling about with an embarrassed looking George, Kara sitting in the old rocking chair, her long dark hair hiding her face as she bent forward, stroking one of the many cats, another in the kitchen with us proudly showing off some dish or other we had concocted.

There was something odd about that photo of Kara, something about the way she was sitting stroking the cat and deliberately avoiding looking at the camera, almost as if she didn't want to be photographed. What was it I hadn't noticed then but was lurking in the back of my mind now?

In the last photo there was something in the far corner, almost out of shot and holding it this way and that, I peered at it closely.

Almost hidden from view, in the furthest part of the kitchen sat Gabriel, narrow-eyed, watching us all, brooding like some dark avenging angel, unaware he'd been captured on film. A shiver ran down my spine. Was I never to be free of this ghost?

Seeing him like that, seeing Kara so still, jolted my memory yet again as though by a series of small electric shocks, each one triggering another memory.

To my horror, this time the picture that flashed before my eyes was what had happened the night Kara made her suicide attempt.

THIRTEEN

It was Melanie who found her. Josie might have become hysterical, but fortunately she wasn't in the house at the time and Melanie remained as cool and collected as ever.

She was found only because Melanie had gone in to pay her rent, not something any of us did with any frequency. In theory the rent was due promptly on the first of each month, in practice no one kept to that arrangement because Kara was far too tolerant of us all. It was more like being part of a family, rather than a landlady-tenant relationship.

The way she looked after me was a good example of her kindness. After a few months on Melanie's camp bed and with no success in finding a place of my own, at least not anything affordable on my tiny income, Kara took pity on me and cleared out the smaller of the rooms on the top floor.

Because my room was so cramped compared to the others and it was only a "temporary" arrangement, Kara said, 'There's no rush to find a place, Alison - stay here with us. It's such a basic room; half rent will more than cover the costs.'

Aware of how kind she had been to squeeze yet one more person into her crowded life, my conscience did trouble me if I didn't pay on time, so I was never more than a day or two late. And I was genuinely grateful she'd made me feel welcome. If I'd had to spend one more Friday morning rushing out to get the *Ham and High* and spend hours cramped in a local phone box watching my money rapidly disappear on calls to all the adverts for bedsits, I'd as soon have packed up and gone back to Glasgow.

By one of those strange coincidences, Melanie had gone to pay Kara very late at night because she was going off on a course the next day, one of many arranged for those considered "high flyers" by her employer.

She searched for Kara downstairs and when she didn't find her in her usual place by the fire in the kitchen, she decided she'd better try her room, though it was most unlike Kara to go to bed early. Often you would come back late at night and find her prowling the house like one of her cats, or sitting gazing at the dying embers of the fire in the kitchen.

As for me, I'd started a temporary job with a firm of solicitors in Maida Vale by this time and though only a few weeks into the job, was absolutely shattered by the work after months of complete idleness.

So, exhausted by this unaccustomed effort, I'd been in bed for some time and was drifting off to sleep when a loud knock on the door startled me into wakefulness.

'Alison, get up. Come and help me.'

Believing this to be no more than a dream, I turned over and snuggled back down under the blankets. Another knock - louder this time, more insistent.

'Alison, can you hear me? Come quickly.'

The incessant pounding on the door: no dream, but the stuff of nightmares.

In that groggy state between sleeping and waking, I stumbled around in the half dark, trying to find my slippers by touch.

'What's the matter?' I yawned, struggling with the door, trying all the while to pull my dressing gown round me. 'Is it a fire?'

The sight of Melanie's face, ashen and wide eyed, was enough to convince me this really was an emergency.

'What's wrong Melanie? What is it?' Now fully alert, I grabbed her by the arm and shook her.

She gasped a little and finally managed to say, 'It's Kara. There's something wrong, she won't answer the door.'

Together we went across the landing to Kara's room, terrified at what we might find, and stood listening intently, neither of us with any idea what to do next.

'Can you hear anything?' I whispered to Melanie who had her ear pressed up against the door.

Melanie shook her head. She was as frightened as I was. 'I know she's in there,' she said. 'We'll have to try to break in.'

This didn't sound a good idea. 'What if ...well... if she doesn't want to talk to us?' I ventured timidly.

Melanie was having none of my cowardice. 'For goodness sake, Alison,' she hissed, 'even if she's not keen to be disturbed she's surely not going to sit in there and listen to us banging the door for hours on end. She would do something if she was able to, even only to tell us to go away.'

'I suppose so,' I agreed reluctantly.

While what Melanie said made a lot of sense, I'd have preferred it if someone else had been summoned to deal with the problem.

'There's nothing else for it. Here goes.' Melanie took a deep breath, pushed her hair back from her face and banged loudly on the door again and again, but there was still no reply, no response. She rattled the handle but it refused stubbornly to budge. 'Damn, she's locked it,' she said in a low voice.

It did occur to me that if we were banging so loudly on the door to waken Kara, there was absolutely no point in talking in whispers outside. Why on earth was Kara not responding?

'Perhaps she's not there, she's gone out somewhere.'

'Oh, for goodness sake, Alison, who's locked the door from the inside then? Unless of course you think she locked the door from inside and then hotfooted it out the window.'

Suitably chastened, I bit my lip. Melanie sounded upset, a sign she was very worried.

The noise we were making may not have disturbed Kara, but it wakened George and he came crashing up the stairs to see what was going on, scratching his tousled hair and yawning. 'What's all the din about? Is it burglars or what?'

'We can't get any reply from Kara,' said Melanie, gnawing at her lower lip anxiously.

George yawned again and shrugged his shoulders. 'Maybe she isn't in,' he said. 'Have you thought of that?'

Melanie glared at him. Two people making the same inane comment was too much for her.

'You'll have to break the door down, George.'

He looked most reluctant and a bit sheepish.

'What if, you know, she's in there with someone ...?'

'Oh, don't be so silly, George,' Melanie interrupted him. 'Even if she was in the middle of a passionate night, she'd have heard us banging on the door like this. Why are we standing here wasting time?'

He put a restraining hand on her arm.

'Steady on, Melanie. I want to make sure that we're not over-reacting.'

Melanie shouted at him, 'George, do something!'

'Well, I suppose so, Melanie, but I'm not taking the blame if it all goes wrong.'

She gave him a push. 'Go on,' she insisted. 'We're wasting time standing here talking about it.'

'Try once more,' he said.

When that failed, he put his shoulder to the door. At least all that public school rugby proved useful for something, but even with George's strength and Melanie and I giving what assistance we could, it took some effort. These Victorian doors were solidly built and not designed to be moved easily.

There was the sound of splintering wood, the door gave way with a groan and we all fell into the room, Melanie first. We stood together in shocked silence, trying to make sense of what we could see.

Kara was lying on her side on the bed, looking as if she was no more than sound asleep. It was only when you looked more closely and saw the strange angle she was at, the empty tablet bottle on the floor beside her, that you realised this was no ordinary sleep.

George and I stood stock still, unable to move, but Melanie efficiently took control. 'Go and phone for an ambulance. Quickly!' she screamed in my face as I continued to stand there staring. She turned to George. 'Come over here and help me,' she commanded.

At last spurred into action, I ran downstairs to the telephone in the hall and with trembling fingers dialled 999.

'Emergency: which service do you require?' came the clipped voice. For a moment I couldn't speak, but eventually managed to get the words out after a couple of attempts and had been assured "help is on its way," I rushed back upstairs.

'They'll be here as soon as possible,' I gasped, but George and Melanie weren't listening: they were too busy trying to rouse Kara from her drugged stupor by walking her up and down the room.

Never having encountered anything like this before, I'd no idea what to do, or even if George and Melanie were doing the right thing, so I crept out and went downstairs to wait for the ambulance at the window in Melanie's room, the one which faced the overgrown garden, willing someone to arrive.

Help arrived very quickly, though to me it seemed like years before there was the welcome sound of that bell clanging up the street and I was able to open the door to the ambulance men with an overwhelming sense of relief. Surely now everything would be all right?

It was frightening to see them bring Kara back downstairs on a stretcher, tightly wrapped in a blanket.

'Do you want me to come with you to the hospital?' I asked Melanie, and was ashamed at my feeling of relief when she shook her head.

'It'll be less trouble if only one of us goes. I'll give you a ring and let you know what's happening.' And with that she was off in the ambulance with Kara.

By now Josie had arrived from the late night film at the *Everyman* cinema up in Hampstead and it took some time to calm her down. She kept on repeating, 'What happened, what happened?' but as none of us knew the answer, there was little to tell her.

With Kara and Melanie gone, there was nothing we could do for now but wait for news and we went downstairs into the kitchen, seeking comfort in familiar surroundings. Sleep was of course out of the question. We were all too fraught and worried to feel tired.

George looked at me. 'Was it an accident, Alison?'

I gave a shrug of my shoulders. What did I know?

'Do you think she'll be all right?' asked Josie in a little frightened voice.

'Of course she will. I'm sure we found her in time,' I replied briskly, with a lot more conviction than I felt. 'More tea, anyone?' I refilled the teapot for something to do, to keep me busy, though none of us wanted more tea.

Suddenly Josie stopped snuffling into her handkerchief. 'Where's Gabriel?' she said, looking round.

In all the excitement, we'd completely forgotten about him.

'I'll check his room,' said George, 'but I don't see how he could have slept through all the noise that's been going on, could he?'

Neither of us tried to stop him. We were weary, but not tired, and there was that peculiar sense of time moving incredibly slowly while we waited for Melanie to phone with news of Kara.

George came scrambling back downstairs into the kitchen a few minutes later.

'Well, that explains why he heard nothing. He's scarpered.'

Josie stared at George, as though finding it difficult to understand what he was saying.

'What makes you think he's gone?'

'The place is so clear. There are none of his belongings around as far as I can see.'

'I'll take a look.'

Josie got up from the table. She returned quickly, shaking her head.

'No sign of him, but it's difficult to tell. I've no idea what his room looks like normally.'

George glared at her as if to say, 'I told you so,' but at least he had the sense not to make matters worse by saying it out loud.

We knew what she meant. None of us had been inside Gabriel's room so it would be impossible to know if this was its usual state. The surprise was that it had been unlocked.

Every time I looked at my watch it seemed scarcely another second had passed, and at one point George, equally on edge, suggested we might phone the hospital. None of us knew which hospital she'd been taken to, and no one wanted to be the one to make the phone call. If the news was bad, we'd know all about it soon enough.

We continued to sit around aimlessly, our questions hanging in the air unspoken while we willed the phone to ring or Melanie to return from the hospital with some word about what was happening to Kara.

The minutes crept into hours and still there was no news. As we sat in that silent house in Hampstead, there was one thought in everyone's mind.

Had Gabriel really disappeared and, if he had, was it anything to do with Kara's suicide attempt? Unless, of course, it was something even more sinister than that.

FOURTEEN

As quickly as they had begun, the festive holidays came to an end.

Gerry was the first to leave on Boxing Day, pleading pressure of work, though it was my suspicion several days of frantic family life had been more than enough for him. He's a confirmed bachelor who likes his own space, his neat and tidy life.

The children departed for their various flats in a whirl of lost keys, misplaced shoes and bulging suitcases, leaving a lingering trail of promises to write and to phone.

If my own New Year resolutions were anything to go by, none of this would happen and I'd spend the next few weeks trotting backwards and forwards to the Post Office, dispatching items they'd forgotten and "needed urgently."

I guiltily took down the last of the decorations the day before returning to work, vowing this year to keep in touch with those friends who were now no more than a brief catch-up note in the Christmas card.

My diary was still missing. Several times I'd been about to ask Simon outright, but somehow my courage always failed me. I'd taken to watching him warily for any signs something suspicious was going on, but there was nothing unusual in his behaviour. If anything, he seemed more cheerful than usual.

More and more I became convinced he only had my best interests at heart and was worried finding the diary might set me back, might cause me to relapse. But now I knew it still existed I had to locate it, no matter what reminders of the past might be lurking in its pages.

As always, school was subdued the first day of term. The post holiday blues are somehow worse after Christmas. Perhaps it's something to do with the dark mornings, dark nights and the arrival of the credit card bills.

Then there's that awful realisation those New Year resolutions you've been making about dieting or getting fit, as you indulge in yet another slice of cake or a glass of wine, now have to be fulfilled.

The treadmill of teaching, preparing and correcting had begun in earnest this term as the final exams loomed and the only consolation was it all left me so exhausted I'd even begun to sleep better, helped greatly by the fact there'd been no more sightings of Gabriel. Even so, I avoided going into town. No point in tempting fate.

By the time we'd lurched towards half term I was more than ready to take up Susie's idea of going to London, but Simon wasn't keen. He hummed and hawed, sidestepped a decision whenever I brought up the subject.

'We'll have to book the train soon, Simon,' I protested two weeks before the break.

There was a moment's hesitation then he said, 'Why don't you go down and visit Maura on your own. Go for the whole week.' He added, 'I'm too busy here. You know the problems at work at the moment. This will give me a chance to catch up.'

I didn't believe him, but wasn't going to say so. 'Well, could you come down for a long weekend,' I persisted, 'and then we could at least travel back together?'

'Alison, I am trying to explain,' he said in that patient tone of voice he sometimes adopts, 'I'm right in the middle of the most crucial stage of work. The future of the department depends on the right decision being made.'

Unconvinced it was as simple as he claimed, I made no attempt to disguise my disbelief.

He went on, 'It's our busiest time, right before the end of the financial year. Dearly though I'd love to come with you, I can't get away. And there are other problems to deal with.'

'Admit it; you don't want to go back to London.' I resorted to my martyred expression.

'Honestly, Alison, I can't spare the time.'

Though his reasons for needing to remain in Glasgow sounded perfectly plausible, there was a little niggle of doubt in my mind and it was very strange indeed that he didn't ask why I was insisting on this trip. I'd said no more to him about the Gabriel incident, convincing myself it was too late to start now.

I wanted answers, and had this feeling deep down that returning to where it all happened would somehow help me exorcise my ghosts. Nothing else seemed to be helping me find out the truth.

There was no point in any further discussion: Simon was resolute. Better to go along with his decision.

'Sorry, Simon, I do understand. And no one is forcing me to go. I'll be fine. There's plenty to do in London.'

'Fly down, Alison, or travel first class. That way you'll enjoy the journey,' he said, making it clear there would be no way of changing his mind.

We returned to a more amicable state. After all, it was my choice to go. I could have stayed at home and made a more determined effort to forget all about Gabriel, though that would be easier said than done.

The trouble was, instead of dealing with those memories from long ago, I'd been trying to suppress them, had this irrational belief that finding out the truth about Gabriel held the key to restoring my peace of mind.

Simon was right about one thing. There was no reason not to go on my own. In fact the more I thought about it the more sensible it seemed. And I'd had one or two prompts from Susie, not to mention the occasional remark from Harry like, 'Seen any good videos lately, Alison?' which I did my best to ignore.

So it was decided. After Simon had left for college, I sat nursing my cup of coffee for a precious few minutes before making ready for school.

Half term was still over a week away, but at lunchtime I'd head for the local travel agent's to book my ticket, knowing he'd give me a good price as he does so much business with the school. I set off to work in a much more relaxed, if not exactly happier, frame of mind.

Immediately after break I'd a free period and was sitting at the table by the window, trying to make some sense of the essay submitted by one of the less able third year boys when a breathless Susie burst into the room, like a charge of electricity, her hair and her clothes equally dishevelled.

'Hi, Alison, thought I might catch you.'

She threw herself down into the nearest chair and lay back. 'Whew! I'm absolutely whacked. What a day! Why do none of my pupils have less than three problems each?'

I stifled a laugh, saying in a stern voice, 'Not less, fewer, Susie. Remember the old saying: less pudding and fewer potatoes?' I teased her.

'Oh, do shut up, Alison,' she replied good-humouredly, rising to the bait. She lifted the cushion from behind her head and aimed it at me. She missed, but hit Harry Sneddon, as he came shambling into the room, as usual a picture of gloom.

'For goodness sake, act your age you two,' he said by way of greeting, lifting the cushion from the floor.

He wasn't in the best of moods these days. The school had been unable to find a suitable temporary replacement for him and his refresher course had been postponed, much to his annoyance. School policy, fair enough, is that we all have our share of difficult classes. Susie and I exchanged raised eyebrows over his bent back.

'What's with you, Harry?' said Susie in her usual blunt fashion, wriggling herself into a more comfortable position.

He looked gloomier than ever.

'I've been given a "please take" slip for 3H last two periods of the afternoon, that's what. Fred's off again. In fact he's off more often than he's actually here.'

Harry evidently considered this was adding insult to injury, that someone had found an alternative way of escape.

We both groaned in sympathy. There's nothing worse than having to take someone else's class at short notice, especially if it's a class like 3H: adolescent boys with no interests except football. Harry left, laden with a pile of exercise books, muttering to himself.

'Well, Alison,' said Susie after he'd gone, 'what's to do with this ghost you saw recently. Any further forward?'

'Not really,' I said, reluctant to enter into yet another discussion. In truth, I was beginning to be sorry I'd mentioned this business of Gabriel to Susie - every time I saw her it was an unspoken question, even if she didn't talk openly about it.

I hadn't mentioned seeing Gabriel at the Theatre Royal: that would only make matters worse. Susie would probably ask me why I hadn't confronted him, even had it meant lying down in the road in front of the taxi. Had I been obsessed about seeing him to the extent of superimposing his face on some complete stranger in the theatre? Someone who bore no more than a passing resemblance to him? And why would Melanie be with him?

All I said to Susie was, 'I'm going down to London at half term to see Maura, so I might take up your suggestion of looking for the death certificate. Simon can't make it, so I'm going on my own. That should give me plenty of time to sort it all out.'

Susie looked pleased her advice had been acted on and smiled, 'And if, as I suspect, you do find it, let it rest, Alison, for goodness sake.'

'Yes, Susie,' I replied meekly

'You can tell me all about it when you're back,' she said.

Although I nodded in agreement, how much I would tell her depended on exactly what happened.

FIFTEEN

It was a long time since I'd been in London other than just passing through, when the task had been to find our way out of the heavy traffic as quickly as possible and hurry on to our final destination.

When Maura learned I'd be travelling on my own she sounded very concerned. 'Now remember, Mum, I'll be at Euston to meet you. If I'm delayed, wait and don't move.' This last delivered in a stern tone of voice as if she doubted my ability to follow instructions.

'Yes, Maura I'll do that.'

There's no point in arguing with my daughter nor in saying that London may have changed since I lived there but the buildings haven't moved nor the streets been re- named. Maura always thinks she knows best.

Now everything had been arranged to my satisfaction I was rather looking forward to the train journey and had provided myself with a good selection of books and magazines, though I was too excited to do much reading.

Simon insisted on taking me to the station, no doubt feeling a little guilty about not coming with me, failing to understand I was pleased to be on my own and finding it difficult to disguise the fact.

Fortunately the afternoon train was exceedingly quiet. Only a few weary looking businessmen occupied the compartment, hunched over reports or engrossed in the pages of the *Financial Times*, and I settled in my comfortable seat well away from the draughts of the automatic doors.

'You'll be all right then,' said Simon for the umpteenth time in as many minutes as he fidgeted about, tapping his fingers on the back of my reserved seat.

'Perfectly fine,' I reassured him, catching his hand to stop him. 'Make sure you don't get into any trouble while I'm away.'

'What do you mean by that?' he said abruptly.

'Why, nothing. Only a joke.'

The tone of his reply momentarily startled me.

He tried to cover his tracks.

'Don't worry; I've plenty to do at college.'

We parted with a feeling of dissatisfaction: he gave me a brief kiss and a wave as he left the train.

As soon as he'd disappeared down the platform I settled back with my book, determined to make an attempt at reading, but it was no use. I kept stopping mid sentence, thinking about that article from Maura and what had happened all those years ago in Kara's house, or what might have happened.

Unable to concentrate, I gazed out of the window as we crossed the border and rattled towards London. Flat, flat country. The network South East trains looked almost continental with their livery of grey, red and blue. We were through the vast sprawl of Bletchley in the blink of an eye as we kept up speed, and then outside Leighton Buzzard, where the setting sun reddened the brick houses, I suddenly spied the first real thatched cottage.

In every green field punctuating the towns there were horses. I remembered reading somewhere there are now more horses round London than there were in the Middle Ages.

Signs of industrial activity greeted our arrival at Tring. Now there was the feeling of London stretching out its tentacles as the green spaces between the houses became smaller and smaller and finally vanished altogether till all you could see was the jumble of houses clustered more tightly round the track, huddling together for protection.

By Hemel Hempstead the only green was that of the gardens and through a dark tunnel of trees we arrived in Watford. Not quite as I remembered it: from what I could see while we were stopped briefly at the station, there were a few more plants, a better looking waiting room, but still that air of endurable grime that is the trademark of London for me.

Off again, on down through the suburbs, one indistinguishable from the next in the gathering gloom of the late afternoon. I'd be glad to arrive at my destination.

We drew in to Euston station exactly on time and as I came up the ramp with the other weary travellers, there was Maura at the barrier, frantically waving to me.

She hugged me tightly at the same time as taking my luggage from me and bombarding me with a series of questions. 'How are you, Mum? Great to see you. Had a good journey?'

She shepherded me across the concourse, transformed by the array of shops that had sprung up since I'd last been there, but there was no time to dawdle.

'Alan has brought his car to save us the bother of the Tube journey,' she said as we reached the exit.

Alan? Who was Alan? She hadn't mentioned Alan to me, but I said nothing lest we start off our week together on the wrong foot.

Sure enough a dark blue Volvo was parked by the kerb, its engine running for a quick getaway from the roar of life round the station.

Out into the London traffic: great streams of shining lights in the rush hour, which seemed to go on for ever. Was it really so much noisier than I remembered? As I knew to my cost, memory can play strange tricks and perhaps in those days I wasn't as aware of the noise and the bustle.

Maura chattered non-stop in the car which allowed me to sneak a good look at Alan. He was obviously the strong silent type which was no doubt why he appealed to Maura. In spite of his evidently expensive clothes he wasn't very inspiring.

Then I scolded myself for thinking like this. Maura was well able to make her own choices now. And my daughter was always able to talk enough for at least two people. With a supreme effort I tuned back into what she was saying.

'...and I thought we'd go to see Buckingham Palace, though I'm not sure that it's open to the public at this time of year...'

A feeling of panic seized me as she continued. How on earth would I be able to investigate this business about Gabriel if Maura had lined up a week visiting tourist attractions? Didn't she remember I'd lived in London once?

'Mum!' A cross voice in my ear. 'You're not listening to a word I'm saying.'

'Of course I am,' I said lamely. 'It all sounds really exciting.'

Then I could have bitten my tongue out, annoyed at giving the impression I was agreeing with these exhausting suggestions. How to wriggle out of this rigorous itinerary without offending my daughter? There was absolutely no way I wanted to waste this precious time in London sightseeing, though being honest, at the moment I didn't have much of a plan.

Maura was gazing at me with a look of horror.

'We can't do it all in a week, Mum, you'll be tired out.'

Wrong answer again, it would appear. Perhaps she'd expected me to turn down all these proposals. Sometimes you can't win.

Alan, though not speaking, was nodding furiously in agreement with all that Maura was saying.

Oh dear, what had I let myself in for? I'd be better to pluck up my courage, be decisive, whether Maura was pleased or angry.

'Actually, Maura, I'd prefer not to interfere with your plans,' I said in what I hoped was a tactful manner.

As she looked dubious I hurried on, 'I'm more than happy to wander round on my own, remind myself of old haunts, maybe look up some old friends…' My voice tailed away.

Maura looked astonished at this. 'I didn't know you'd any friends left in London?'

'Well, not really friends as such, but I think one or two people I knew in the old days might still be here. I'd like to try to track them down…' My voice petered out again.

She obviously thought I'd taken leave of my senses to trail all the way down from Glasgow to look up old friends I'd known many years ago who by now might well be in Australia or even Timbuktu, so little contact had I had with them.

'How will you do that? Track them down I mean?'

For a moment I detected a note of sarcasm in that question, or perhaps it was no more than my imagination, my oversensitivity these days.

But I was determined, and that gave me courage. I hadn't come all this way to end up tramping round the usual tourist sights and on this occasion I wasn't going to be bullied by my daughter. It might suit Alan, but it didn't suit me.

When we'd finally negotiated the traffic up the Finchley Road and arrived back at her flat in West Hampstead where Alan dropped us off, I asked her about this new boyfriend.

She laughed loudly. 'Oh, for goodness sake, Mum. He's only a friend. Don't start hearing wedding bells. Things are quite different from they were in your day.' With that she dismissed the subject.

I didn't think things were all that different, but refrained from saying so. In spite of her trendy appearance, my daughter isn't quite as worldly wise as she likes to think she is, but it was better to say no more. If there was romance in the air she would tell me in her own good time.

Maura had prepared supper. I wasn't hungry, but had to try to eat after all the trouble she'd obviously taken to make something I'd enjoy.

It was a delicious meal: home-made pasta with a mushroom and mascarpone sauce, green salad dressed with herbs, fresh ciabatta and Tiramisu for dessert. Not to mention the bottle of excellent Chianti we shared. It was as well Simon wasn't with me, as he might compare my shop bought dried pasta and supermarket sauce a bit unfavourably with this.

We sat and chatted as we ate. It was good to catch up with her in this relaxed way, instead of amid the bustle of one of her usual trips home, but when she saw me yet again trying to stifle a yawn, she stood up and took my glass from my hand.

'I'm boring you rigid or you're absolutely shattered,' she said. 'Either way you'd be better off going to bed and having a good night's sleep.'

This sounded a sensible option, though I was at pains to point out that it was tiredness and not her conversation making me yawn. 'It has been rather a long day,' I admitted.

But no sooner was I snuggled into bed in Maura's minute but tastefully decorated spare room than I was wide awake. Partly it was being in a strange bed, partly being on my own. After years of marriage you find it hard to get used to the space.

I tossed and turned, put the light on and read for a while, then put the light out again for fear Maura would notice and come in to see what was wrong.

I felt hungry, which seemed ridiculous after all I'd eaten, but didn't want to go into the kitchen in case I disturbed her and tried to ignore the rumblings in my stomach. Tomorrow I'd buy a packet of biscuits for such an eventuality. There would be a lot to do and I really needed to sleep.

When I did at last drop off, images floated in and out of my mind. In that half world between sleep and wakefulness I almost imagined myself back in King Henry's Road in Hampstead, ready to scramble up in the morning to make the journey across the city to my first job, as I'd done a thousand times before.

I drifted into sleep to the distant clatter of the tube trains rumbling to and fro, but it was a restless sleep peopled with ghosts and a fear of what the week would bring.

SIXTEEN

The song filtered through my consciousness, jerking me awake, for a moment disorientating me in place as well as time.

As I pulled myself out of sleep, remembering I was in Maura's spare room, I realised the song was coming not from a record player, but from a radio in some other flat close by. It had been warm for the time of year, a lot warmer than in Glasgow, and I must have fallen asleep with the window still slightly open.

The tune was so familiar, yet one I hadn't heard for such a long time. Then as it came again, that refrain of *Crève Salope, Crève Salope*, something clicked in my brain and jolted me awake with a sudden terrible realisation: it was Gabriel's song.

That picture of Gabriel in the rocking chair at Kara's sprang to mind. I'd had no idea then what it was all about, but I knew now. And so did Kara. And his humming of the song was deliberate, to upset her. I wished I'd found out more from that tape of Harry's. It must be something to do with those student riots in Paris. But what exactly? No matter how hard I tried to remember, it was a complete blank.

I swung the pillow round as a backrest and sat up in bed to squint at my watch, unable to believe it was almost nine o' clock. Maura would surely have left for work by now. But just as I was contemplating getting out of bed to check, she knocked at the door and put her head round.

'Morning, Mum. Thought I'd let you sleep for a while. You were obviously very tired.'

The last bars of the song died away and I returned to the present.

'Shouldn't you be at work by now?'

She laughed. 'No, Mum, it's perfectly all right. Don't worry.' Then she added, 'Though I have to admit I've a problem later today.'

She looked at me with a frown, concerned about my reaction.

'There's a crisis meeting about the budget for that new feature I was telling you about. I'll have to be there. Tom rang to say that the client isn't too happy with what we're proposing.'

My heart gave a little leap. Did this mean I was to be spared the tourist trail of London and could sneak off on my own? I tried to look suitably crestfallen so as not to disappoint her.

'Oh, never mind, Maura, I'm sure I'll manage fine. There's plenty for me to do. Remember I lived here once so I do know my way around.'

For good measure I added, 'I'm very capable of finding my own way about and I can ask if there are any difficulties. Anyway, I'll take it easy. I'm still tired after that journey yesterday and the wine we had last night,' I said, lying back on the pillow to give some credibility to my statement.

It must have been a convincing performance or else I sounded unusually determined, because Maura looked relieved at my suggestion.

'As long as you're quite sure, Mum. I hate leaving you alone on your first day.'

'Yes, there's absolutely no problem. You go off and have your meeting. I'll take my time and potter off when I feel like it.'

Maura stood up.

'I've left plenty of food in the kitchen and the spare key is hanging on the peg next to the larder underneath the pin board.'

As she turned to leave, 'I've left my mobile number there as well. Remember to take it with you in case you need to contact me - even if you have to interrupt the meeting.' She was chewing her bottom lip, a sign since childhood she was anxious about something, but I did my best to reassure her. Really, it was all quite ridiculous.

By now I was shooing her away.

'Maura, I'll find what I need and can't possibly think of any emergency that would require me to call you out of an important meeting. Now off you go before you're too late and miss everything.'

'Well, I could do with being in early, there's a lot of preparation to do. This is a very difficult client.'

The flat door slammed a few minutes later and I lay back with a sense of relief. My mind drifted to that song again. How long was it since I'd heard *Crève Salope*? Was it an omen? And if so, was it good or bad?

At least I now knew what it was, but there was still the question about how it was connected to Gabriel, and why it had affected Kara so badly when she heard it.

Suddenly I wondered how Simon was, but it was only a fleeting thought, promising myself to phone him later. And now I'd the whole day in front of me, I wasn't sure where to begin.

Do this in a logical way, I said sternly to myself and jumped out of bed to fetch a notebook and pen from my bag, then sat down in the chair by the window to make a list, or rather several lists.

The first was a list of all the people I remembered as being in the house at the time Gabriel lived there, the second was a list of all the places we'd frequented and the third was a list of the places I might begin to look for information.

I could start with Somerset House, at the Registry of Deaths, as Susie had suggested. Gabriel had been certified dead, had been identified by Kara, and yet here I was in London because I thought I'd seen him twice in Scotland. Yes, the first thing I had to do was find a copy of the death certificate. That was the most important -and might be the only - essential.

Then again, Susie's article could have been correct and I was imagining seeing Gabriel because of some unknown trauma experienced recently. Though that seemed most unlikely: surely nothing at work or at home could have caused such a violent reaction.

After several attempts, I managed to operate the shower in the miniscule bathroom and put on trousers, a thin jumper and some comfortable shoes, remembering how hard the streets of London could be on your feet. I wasn't sure that my elegant daughter would quite approve of my attire, but could always change into something more suitable before she came home.

It would be a better plan to tackle these tasks after some breakfast, but in spite of Maura's assurances about how well stocked her larder was, it was something of a disappointment. I'm not really into muesli or the other complicated cereals she preferred and finally settled for a boiled egg and some toast, with more tea, after wrestling fruitlessly with the instructions for her shiny chrome coffee machine.

Over breakfast I came to a decision: the death certificate could wait a little longer. Firstly I had to return to the street in Hampstead where I'd lived, hoping something there might be familiar, might help me. Remembering was central to the answer about Gabriel, that was for sure.

Half an hour later, suitably fortified and with my capacious handbag packed with a new copy of the *A-Z of London,* plus a fold out Tube map, I lifted the spare key from the hook beside the front door and set forth confidently on my quest.

The Tube station was only a short walk from Maura's flat and even at this time of day it was busy, though it was a pleasant surprise to see how much cleaner and brighter everything was from when I'd last been here. I was down into the bowels of the earth and back up into the sunlight at Swiss Cottage in no time at all.

Once out of the Tube station I hesitated, uncertain whether to turn left or right. Fortunately I made the correct choice and crossed onto Avenue Road and down Adelaide Road to arrive in a few minutes at the end of King Henry's Road. I stood gazing down its length, searching for signs of something recognisable after all the years away. There must be something here to help me make sense of what was happening to me.

Strangely, from this end of the road it was almost exactly as I remembered: a long road of tall Victorian villas where a few straggly trees punctuated the verges and here and there daffodils struggled to maintain existence in the tiny front gardens.

I started to walk slowly down on the shady side of the pavement, realising how I'd been deceived, becoming increasingly amazed at how many changes had taken place. When I'd lived on this street, these villas had been shabby, with peeling paint, rubbish-strewn gardens and a pervading aura of neglect in spite of the best efforts of the few long term residents to maintain some level of respectability. Most had been run down and unloved, divided haphazardly into flats: each one a temporary refuge for students or those starting out who'd discovered the streets of London weren't all paved with gold.

Now I walked slowly past them, dazzled by the shining new paintwork, swagged and tailed curtains adorning the windows, new brass door knobs gleaming in the sunshine. This street had gone decidedly upmarket.

To my amazement the corner shop we'd used on a daily basis (we were always running out of something or other) had become a very trendy coffee bar. Now it was all chrome and skinny latte instead of the jumble of newspapers, toys and Vesta curries favoured by the previous owner.

For a moment I was disorientated and stood looking about me, unable to remember which of these renovated houses had been Kara's. What was the number? How could I forget something like that? Easily, it would appear.

Then I spied it across the street, immediately opposite. The only one that hadn't been renovated. Or rather, was in the process of being renovated.

A large skip, half full of rubble, sat outside the front door and all the windows were wide open. This was better than I'd hoped. I'd been trying to think of all sorts of ploys that would let me gain entry for a look round, but could come up with nothing that sounded even remotely plausible. Here was a golden opportunity.

All I had to do was talk my way past the builders whose van marked *High Style Renovators* was parked half on and half off the pavement. From the windows came the sound of buzzing and hammering accompanied by the tuneless singing of some pop song or other.

Taking a deep breath, I edged my way carefully round the building rubble and the van and walked up to a burly red-haired young man coming out of the front door. 'Excuse me; is there any chance of seeing inside this house?' I asked timidly.

He looked at me doubtfully.

'Sorry, love, there's no point. It's not for sale. We're doing the renovations for the new owner.'

He waved his arm vaguely in the direction of the interior in case I didn't believe what he was saying.

'No, no,' I replied hastily, before he could move off, 'I used to live here and I'd like to see round.' It all sounded very lame, if not highly suspicious.

He scratched his head and regarded me thoughtfully, weighing me up, wondering how to refuse without upsetting me.

'Don't think so, love. The chap that owns it now got it off some old geezer who was his great uncle or summat.'

I shook my head. I wasn't doing a very good job of persuading him, but now was really desperate to see inside. There had to be some way to convince him, so I tried again. 'No, you don't understand. I lived here many years before that - I was a tenant here.'

Still no response. If anything he looked more puzzled than ever.

Before he could refuse me again, I said, 'It belonged to someone called Kara, Kara Redditch, and it was her house.' I stopped, suddenly aware chattering on like this wasn't helping my cause.

He shrugged his shoulders and said, 'Suppose there'd be no harm in it, but I need to check with the gaffer. All the structural work's been done and we're on to the painting now, but still you know, Health and Safety and all that ...'

Sure enough, there was a strong smell of gloss paint wafting out of the building.

'Hold on a minute.'

He put up his hand to stop me as I went to step across the threshold while he was still in a receptive mood. He went back inside.

I heard voices, obviously debating whether I was to be trusted or not and, unable to bear the suspense, craned my neck to hear what they were saying.

The red-headed builder emerged with the gaffer in tow, conferring about me

'Is it all right?' I asked eagerly. 'I'll be really careful.'

The gaffer, a small weedy man I couldn't ever imagine doing any heavy building work, grinned at me, showing a quantity of yellow, nicotine stained teeth.

'I suppose so, love, but you have to be very careful. Don't want you getting paint over your nice clothes.'

Judging by the amount of paint spatter on their overalls, they weren't the most careful of workmen.

'Thank you very much. Any paint on my clothes I'll accept full responsibility for.'

I stepped quickly inside before he could change his mind.

After all those years I was back in Kara's house.

SEVENTEEN

Whispers of ghosts, laughter long gone. I shivered as I slowly crossed the threshold. A deep breath. What would I find? Or recognise?

At first the freshness and the brightness of the place made me blink: my memories were of a dark and gloomy house, but as I gradually became accustomed to the light, my eyes began to focus on the general shape of the hallway. Strip away this new decor and the shell of the building, the shape, the form were as they'd always been.

There was the long narrow hallway with two large rooms to one side, a smaller room at the end and beside that the glass panelled door and the steps leading to the basement kitchen.

The curved and ornate staircase now gleamed white, its brass and wooden handrail polished and burnished. I ran my fingers over it, feeling the smoothness as I walked slowly up to the first floor to the four bedrooms and gigantic bathroom.

At the door of the bathroom I stopped, smiling at the changes the builders had wrought. Everything looked original: the huge roll top bath, the cistern with the high chain pull, the hand basin big enough to bath a baby. What was missing was that arctic chill that had guaranteed you didn't linger long. Part of the problem had been the old pay-as-you-go water heater which gobbled up money frantically, like some hungry ogre, ensuring the bathwater was enough for only the scantiest of bathing experiences.

Another less ornate stair, equally well restored, led to the attic where Kara had her bedroom and where I'd found refuge in the other, tinier room. At the moment the way was blocked by a workman furiously sanding the wooden skirting boards.

One of the painters, the tuneless whistler, perched half way up a ladder on the stairwell, looked at me curiously as I wandered round, peering into corners, occasionally laughing to myself at the memory of some event from long ago.

Now I'd made a preliminary tour of the house I was at a loss. What was I supposed to do next?

There had been no earth-shattering revelation, no heart-stopping memory to explain the problem about Gabriel.

The young painter put me out of my misery by breaking into my thoughts.

'Used to live here then, did you? Bet it cost a lot less then than it does now.'

He waved his paint brush in an alarming manner and I swiftly moved aside to dodge any paint spatter.

'Don't mind us. You have a good look round.'

He was probably under the impression I'd once been the owner of the place, come to see how my investment had prospered. He went back to his painting and his tuneless whistling.

More confident now, I decided to make a thorough search of the house, take it step by step. This might well be my only opportunity and my plan was to go through each room in turn, hoping for some clue. I went downstairs, back to the entrance, determined to conduct this search in a methodical way.

Gingerly I pushed open the door to the first room on the ground floor, trying to see it as it had been, not as it was now. This had been Melanie's room, but the psychedelic posters and the purple decor had all been swept away and the room restored to its former glory. Had it always had this beautiful ornate cornice and wooden panelling, or was it a modern restoration? If so, it was cleverly done, because everything looked original.

This was where I'd slept on a put-you-up until Kara had taken pity on me and given me the tiny room at the top of the house. Not only had the room changed beyond recognition, but the garden that had once been a tangle of neglected rosebushes and weeds was now in the process of a very expensive makeover: evident from the pergola, the decking and the half finished pond set among formal flower beds.

A bitter frustration seized me. What had I expected to find? It certainly wasn't this. No trace remained of our presence: it was as though we'd never been here. These rooms were as cool and remote from the rooms of my memory they might well have been from another planet.

None of the other rooms yielded any secrets, not even the basement kitchen where we'd spent so much time together. Unfortunately it was in such a state of disruption I could do no more than stand at the top of the stairs and peer down while one of the workmen hovered beside me anxiously, lest I should come to harm on the steep stairs.

This was hopeless, I thought, beginning to climb the main stairs again. All traces of our lives had been swept away, disposed of in the skips outside.

For a few moments I wandered round the room on the first floor that had been George's. One of the remaining rooms had been Josie's, but I couldn't recollect which, and the other had been a spare room. Suddenly it all came back to me. This room was where Gabriel had lived when he'd come back and though I hadn't been in his room to the best of my recollection, surely it had had a makeover in keeping with the rest of the house.

At the foot of the last set of stairs leading up to the attic rooms I paused, wondering if there was any point in going further, in climbing these stairs again.

There was nothing here for me, nothing to help me in my quest, but the workman had disappeared, the way was clear and besides it would only take a few minutes. After coming all this way it would be foolish not to double check everything.

After another quick look I'd leave and treat myself to a large cappuccino and a croissant or two in that new cafe on the corner that had once been our local grocery shop.

Slowly I climbed this final set of stairs. They seemed a lot steeper than before, leaving me out of breath as I reached the top to push open the door in front of me.

This had been Kara's room. Here I suppose I'd expected a renovation in keeping with the rest of the house: white walls, Laura Ashley curtains, soft carpeting.

To my astonishment this room hadn't been touched, had probably been used as a lumber room after Kara died and the house was sold. The renovators hadn't reached here.

There was no furniture, but the room was to all appearances exactly as when it had been Kara's bedroom. The swirly blue and green patterned wallpaper was now tattered and torn, the floor partly covered by the original striped rug, frayed and dirty, and lying in the corner on its side was the picture of the Eiffel Tower brought back by Melanie as a gift from her first trip abroad.

With a jolt I realised this picture didn't belong here in Kara's room. It had hung in another part of the house.

Then I remembered, the memories came flooding back. Except I didn't want to remember this.

EIGHTEEN

The red-haired workman's words rang in my ears as I fled from the house.

'All right, love? Got what you wanted?'

It was as much as I could do to call out a brief thanks as I ran down the path and out on to the street, only slowing down as I came near the new cafe on the corner. In spite of the tempting smell of the freshly baked *pain au chocolat* I finally selected, I couldn't force it down: with every bite my stomach heaved.

Anxious not to draw attention to myself, as though that mattered in London, I'd bought a paper from the seller on the corner, but did no more than turn the pages, unable to take anything in. How could I have forgotten something so important? Quite easily, it would appear.

I couldn't remember the exact date but it must have been several months after Simon and I had decided our relationship was serious. November, yes, it must have been November, because we'd had an unexpected snowfall. By then I'd given up the job with the solicitors and had found a job working in the library at Swiss Cottage as an assistant. With my new found wealth I'd moved into more comfortable accommodation. Kara had asked me to look out for a copy of Jeanne Houston's *Farewell to Manzanar*, and I decided to drop it off on my way back to my flat.

When I arrived at Kara's there was no reply to my knock (the doorbell had never worked), but I pushed at the door knowing it wasn't often locked, because someone was always losing or forgetting their keys.

'Hi,' I called out, walking slowly along the hall, listening for a response.

There was no answer, but I could hear voices from the basement kitchen and was about to breeze down when something made me pause and proceed more quietly.

At the bottom of the stairs my first sight was of Simon and Josie sitting at the table with their backs to me, their heads close together in an intimate way that took me by surprise.

As I was about to announce my presence with a cheery greeting Simon suddenly leaned over and took Josie's hand in a very tender way, leaving me rooted to the spot. What was going on between them? It looked very much as if he was cheating on me. And with Josie. It was hard to believe, yet here was the evidence.

They must suddenly have been aware of my presence, because they both looked round at the same time, jumping guiltily apart. While I tried to act normally, pretending not to notice anything amiss, I caught Simon nodding a warning to Josie as she started to speak.

He stood up and came over to kiss me.

'Just visiting,' I said brightly, 'and dropping off this for Kara,' as I put the book down on the table.

Simon stood up.

'I'll come back with you.'

'No need,' I replied biting my lip and turning away to hide the tears welling up in my eyes.

Josie said nothing. She sat there, staring down at the table, deliberately not meeting my gaze.

Simon was insistent. 'Take care, Josie,' he said as he steered me upstairs to the front door.

Back in the hall he turned me to face him and took my hands in his.

'Look, Alison, it's not what you think. There's nothing going on between Josie and me. I love you. You have to believe that. Someday I'll be able to explain properly.'

Being young and in love, what was I to do? I trusted him, but perhaps that had been the wrong decision. It certainly explained why he'd so readily remembered Josie and forgotten the others.

Something told me this was a vital part of the puzzle, but no matter how hard I tried I couldn't remember what had happened after that. I felt sick and faint.

When the early lunchtime crowds began to fill the cafe and the waitress had been over twice to ask me if I wanted anything else, there was no option but to leave. I stood up carefully, but fortunately my legs weren't quite as wobbly as they'd been earlier.

Now, more than ever, I was determined to track down Gabriel's death certificate, so clutching the trusty *A-Z of London*, I managed to make my way to Somerset House and even find the right department without too much difficulty.

The whole process was so much easier than anticipated, thanks to the helpful assistant on duty at the desk. Here it was: Gabriel's death certificate. Firm evidence Gabriel was well and truly dead.

I read it and re-read it from the comfort of Maura's sofa, wriggling my toes to ease the tension in my feet. There were few details, but death was clearly by drowning and there was absolutely nothing to indicate it had been anything but an accident. Other details were equally sparse, nothing that would help me track him down if he was still alive.

At the sound of Maura's key in the lock I hastily folded the copy and stuffed it into my handbag and by the time she came into the room was lying back on the sofa, moving my feet about to cool them.

She burst into the room in that energetic way she has, seeming to fill all the space.

'Hi, Mum, with a kiss on the cheek, 'had a good day?'

And almost in the same breath, 'Don't lie there for too long. Alan's coming to take us out to dinner in half an hour. He's managed to book a table at *Les Voyagueses*.'

As she saw the look on my face she went on, 'It's a little restaurant up in Hampstead Village. We've a table reserved for eight o' clock. It gets really crowded because it's so popular, but Alan knows the manager so they've managed to squeeze us in at short notice. I'm sure you'll enjoy it.'

She turned to go adding, 'Oh, by the way I spoke to Dad today. He's anxious to know how you are.' She wagged her finger at me. 'He says you haven't been in touch, haven't replied to his messages. I told him I was looking after you, taking you to a posh place for dinner tonight.'

'Of course, I'll phone him later,' I said hastily, unwilling to be involved in a long explanation about my lack of communication.

What I really wanted was a takeaway pizza in front of the telly and a chat with Maura about nothing in particular. Besides, given Alan's conversation level, which appeared to be almost non-existent, a whole evening in his company was unlikely to be the pleasant event she anticipated. Then again, perhaps Maura's chatter would be enough for all of us. And it would be churlish to complain when she was trying so hard to make sure my visit was enjoyable.

As so often had seemed to happen to me of late, it turned out to be a much more interesting evening than I could ever have imagined.

NINETEEN

We arrived at the restaurant in good time, as it was no more than ten minutes' walk from Maura's flat, sparing us the usual "which one of us drives" scenario. Not that I'd have attempted to drive in the London traffic unless there'd been a real emergency.

Anticipating a week of tramping the London streets or chilling out at Maura's, I'd very little to wear suitable for an evening at a smart restaurant and in the end made do with a black skirt and a rather garish blouse, packed at the last minute in case the weather turned hot.

Maura was right. The restaurant was busy, jammed with people, at least one or two of whom looked vaguely familiar.

'Look, that's Henry Cummings over there,' she whispered in my ear as we went in. When I looked blank, she went on, 'You know, that chap who comperes *Your Turn Next*, the game show on television.'

I watch very little television as I'm usually too busy in the evenings marking essays and my idea of luxury time in front of the T.V. is a good film. Not wanting to disappoint her, because this was obviously the in place to be, I put on a dawning-light-of-recognition face and said (hopefully sounding excited enough), 'Oh, of course, that's who he is.'

She steered me through the front tables, all the while hissing names of apparently well known celebrities in my ear, but by now I'd learned my lesson and put on a look of interest no matter what she said, nodding in feigned surprise each time. Fortunately the lighting was dim.

It did strike me that close up and with little or no make-up, these personalities looked no more glamorous than I did and was considerably cheered up by the time we reached our table. Even better, my worries about a dearth of conversation proved to be completely unfounded.

My idea of a night out is to have a good meal, one that is not too unpredictable, in a quiet spacious setting where you can have a proper conversation, but without every word being overheard because the tables are so close together. *Les Voyagueses* was none of these.

To start with it was so tiny that you could have walked past it without noticing it, especially as it was in a converted basement flat, or so it appeared, of a size to accommodate a dozen tables at most though almost double that number was crammed in.

'Isn't this great,' whispered Maura. 'Alan did well to secure a table at such short notice.'

I merely nodded, not wanting to tell an outright lie. It was the kind of place where the tables themselves were so tiny you had to get on well with your eating companions if you wanted to survive the night.

There were the obligatory stripped wooden floorboards and the white roughcast walls to give the illusion of French provincial, accentuated by a collection of bizarre ornaments whose origin as French was highly dubious. And no one was likely to overhear any conversation as the music was being belted out at a level of decibels even I found too loud.

The choice of music was strange: old Johnny Halliday records and the occasional Jacques Brel. Judging by the number of times they played the same records during the evening, the collection seemed to be limited.

We were given a table in the corner and I selfishly chose the best seat with my back to the wall. Not only did it have a good view of everyone in the restaurant, but it gave me a feeling of security and, as an added bonus, was near the window in the direct line of a cooling breeze, much needed as the temperature in the room was stiflingly hot.

In spite of my reservations, the food was very good and certainly adventurous for me. On Alan's recommendation I tried the snails, something I'd never have attempted without his persuasion, though the safety of the lemon tart was my choice of dessert.

As expected, Alan didn't say much, but Maura chattered nineteen to the dozen about everything and anything between the pauses in the music and the food. We all had a fair amount to drink: Alan could certainly choose wine, I'll say that for him.

Then I heard it. Strange I didn't notice it at first as Maura was in the middle of recounting a very funny story about one of her clients and the effort to concentrate cut out any other noise. But as she came to the end of her story, the last notes of *Crève Salope* died away. My heart began to thump: ridiculous really. It was only a song.

'Something wrong?'

Aware that Maura was looking at me with a worried expression I laughed.

'No, nothing at all. Thought I recognised that tune, that's all.'

But it was unsettling, another reminder. For the rest of the evening I kept expecting to hear it again, was half listening for it, but it wasn't played.

We were at the coffee stage, accompanied by a digestif of brandy (not my usual drink) and feeling quite mellow when a voice beside me said, 'Alison Graham, surely it isn't you?'

I haven't been known by that name since my marriage, but the voice was enough to startle me. I looked up and standing by my chair was a woman who appeared to be about my own age, someone I didn't recognise at all.

But on a second look there was something familiar about her, but I couldn't for the life of me say who she was. She was slim, with fashionably bobbed dark hair and dressed in an expensive black trouser suit discreetly enhanced by a silver chain at her neck. Who would I know like that? Perhaps she had made a mistake. Yet she knew my maiden name.

She smiled, rather pleased it seemed, that while she knew me, I didn't have a clue who she was.

'Don't you remember me, Alison? I know it's been a long time, but surely I haven't changed all that much. You certainly haven't.'

This was said with the air of someone who knows she has changed - and for the better. I stood up, partly out of politeness and partly to have a better look, still racking my brains and certainly not flattered she thought me still as gauche as all those years ago.

'It's me, Josie, don't you remember. I was one of the tenants at Kara's house in Hampstead.' She threw her head back and laughed, displaying a set of pearl white Hollywood teeth. 'Of course that was some time ago.'

Josie, of course it was Josie, but now so unlike the dumpy bespectacled Josie I'd known I'd have walked past her in the street without giving her a second glance, in spite of knowing her so well all those years ago.

Now that she'd announced who she was, I began to see a glimpse of the person I'd once known, but could hardly lie or say, 'Of course I realised it was you,' so made do with, 'Josie! How good to see you again after all this time. You look absolutely terrific.'

'Will you join us?' I asked, though that would have been difficult given the lack of space.

I was saved from this problem as she motioned to her companion hovering in the background. He was considerably younger, sleek and fair haired.

'Sorry, Alison, Justin and I are going on to Quincy's. You know the gallery on Bond Street? There's a new exhibition there that we want to see. We've been meaning to go along for ages.'

She smiled again. 'So while I can't stop now why don't we get together? How about meeting up soon? Where are you living in London?'

I briefly explained I now lived back in Glasgow and was visiting my daughter. I didn't say why, though I was sorely tempted to launch into the whole story.

'If you have time, it would be great to meet for a coffee or lunch,' I said eagerly. This was my chance to re-visit the past and to find out what Josie knew about Gabriel. There was no way I was going to let this opportunity slip.

'Great idea.'

She sounded genuinely enthusiastic as she opened her dinky designer handbag.

'Here's my card. Come over to the office for twelve o'clock tomorrow and we'll go for a long gossipy lunch together.' She sounded genuine in her desire to meet up with me.

'Will that be all right?' I said, somewhat concerned, remembering my own meagre allowance of one hour at school.

'Yes,' she said and again I saw a flash of the old Josie in her smile. 'What's the point of being your own boss if you can't take time off?'

There was no opportunity for further talk because Justin suddenly appeared at her elbow and slid his arm round her waist.

'Come on, honey, we have to go now. The others will be waiting.'

Josie turned and looked at him adoringly and I could see why. Was that a little stab of jealousy? I certainly felt like a country cousin beside this cool and very sophisticated woman.

She turned to Justin.

'Yes, just coming, but it's not often that you have the chance to meet an old friend.'

She grasped my hand and looked into my eyes.

'Now, make sure you come along tomorrow, Alison. We've such a lot to catch up on.'

'I wouldn't miss it, Josie,' I replied. Little did she know wild horses wouldn't have kept me away.

'Who was that?' Maura could hardly contain her curiosity and even Alan looked unusually interested.

I apologised for not introducing them, explaining I'd been too surprised to observe the social niceties, while trying to dismiss the encounter as if it were of little consequence.

'Oh, someone I knew when I lived in London years ago. She was one of the people who lived in that house in Hampstead, with Kara. Her name is Josie.'

Even as I spoke, I realised this woman was as different from the Josie of all those years ago as the proverbial chalk is from cheese. What a stroke of luck to meet up with her like that and even better that she'd recognised me.

For the rest of the evening it was impossible to concentrate. Josie might, or might not, prove to be a source of information, but she was one of the few leads I'd managed to find and might even know what had happened to the others.

Alan paid the (to my mind) extremely large bill without batting an eyelid and we went out into the cool night air. On the walk back to Maura's flat I felt my head clear a little and by the time we reached her entrance all my tiredness had gone, leaving me feeling wide awake. Sleep would be impossible.

When we reached the main entrance to the flat Alan refused the offer of a nightcap and left, giving her no more than a peck on the cheek. He gave me a half bow as he said goodnight. Mothers can be so inhibiting.

Fortunately Maura was in no mood to talk, declaring herself to be exhausted.

'I've another really heavy day tomorrow again, Mum - an early meeting and then two clients to see. Do you mind if I go straight to bed?'

Perhaps she was feeling guilty she wasn't paying me enough attention, but I hastened to reassure her.

'Not at all, Maura, I'll head off to bed too. Don't rush back tomorrow night. Remember I'm meeting Josie and I think I'll have a trip to Oxford Street, do some shopping. '

Hopefully talking to Josie would give me some leads to help me make use of the little time left in London.

Once settled in bed I tried to read my book in an effort to make myself sleepy, but couldn't focus on the plot. After rereading the same page several times I gave up, switched the light off and lay there in the dark, my mind going over and over possible scenarios for the next day until I must have eventually drifted off.

There were so many questions. Was it possible Josie might know the truth about Kara? And as she'd been living in the house at the time, know why Gabriel had left, what he'd been doing in Paris among the student rioters. And most importantly, know why he'd returned?

TWENTY

'There's a message from Dad on the answering machine,' Maura announced the next morning as we sat together drinking coffee.

'I'll speak to him later,' I replied with no intention of doing so. I wanted some answers before telling Simon what I'd been up to.

By now my *A-Z of London* was well thumbed and proved a valuable investment in finding Josie's office in an obscure corner of Holborn, through a very narrow entrance which opened out into a huge glass complex, crowded with a wealth of greenery more suited to a jungle.

A waterfall cascaded down one of the walls, tumbling and splashing into a large stone basin where some rather fierce looking fish darted about. This air of casual elegance didn't come cheap and no doubt the complex, built over an old courtyard, had cost a lot of money. Josie must be doing well to have premises here.

The thought of our meeting had made me almost sick with excitement, unable to eat the breakfast Maura had made. She commented anxiously as I left her flat, 'Are you sure you're not overdoing it? London can be very tiring, you know.'

'No, I'm fine.' Then, to change the subject, 'You will remember to phone Deborah today, won't you? I'm worried about her giving up that course at college so suddenly and perhaps she'll tell you what's really going on.'

'Yes, yes, I promise to give her a ring and report back this evening.'

Now here I was, about to meet with Josie, someone I hadn't seen for so many years. How do you catch up on such a long silence over a lunch break? I'd spent my time on the journey trying to think of suitable questions, but it was as though my mind was paralysed.

I stepped through the automatic doors into the glittering foyer, all marble and chrome like some Art Deco film set and somewhat timidly approached the receptionist. She couldn't have been more than twenty, but had the veneer of someone much older, giving the impression she'd been selected for her ability to intimidate clients.

She looked up from examining her nails. 'Yes?' she said, in a bored voice.

'I've come to see Josie Steadman,' I said, with a confidence I didn't feel.

She raised her perfectly groomed eyebrows.

'Have you an appointment?'

This reply made it obvious it wasn't likely someone like me had an appointment here, but this had the effect of making me angry, dispelling my lack of courage. 'Yes,' I said firmly. 'I suggest you ring through. My name is Alison Cameron.'

Perhaps she wasn't used to being dealt with so abruptly because without another word she lifted the phone, then confirmed in a rather huffy manner, 'Take the lift to the third floor, turn right and it's the fourth door on the left.'

She added as I turned to leave, 'There's a large sign *Creative Directions* on the main door. You can't miss it.' She went back to studying her nails.

The lift was all chrome and glass, with carpeted walls and floor, the ride up was so noiseless as to be unnerving and a few minutes later I stepped out into a long corridor, almost an extension of the lift with its thick carpets and fluted wall lights.

All was silent. There was no one in sight. This was not what I called an office, but I followed the directions the receptionist had given me and after only one wrong turn came to a door with a solid brass plaque on it which read *Creative Directions*.

As I raised my hand to knock, the door opened as if by magic and I found myself in Josie's office. Or rather, I found myself face to face with Josie's secretary, a smartly dressed middle-aged woman whose welcoming smile made her much less intimidating than the dragon downstairs.

I was ushered in to see Josie, only to be shepherded out just as quickly, before I'd the chance to take in more than a vague impression of a minimalist space with only a desk, a couple of chairs and a large bookcase. 'I've booked a table for us across the road. The food's not bad and it's very convenient,' she said.

'Sounds great,' I said, putting on my brightest smile and meekly following her out and down to the ground floor in the noiseless lift. In spite of her warm welcome, there was a tension between us and conversation was limited to an exchange of pleasantries as we went left the building.

The deafening noise of the traffic made conversation impossible and I kept close behind Josie as she calmly (or so it seemed to me) walked out into the rush of cars and buses to cross the road.

This restaurant Josie had chosen was better than the one we'd been in the night before. It was much quieter, for one thing and though there was background music, it was light and muted. It was a popular meeting place, judging by the crowd, and as soon as we went in the manager came bustling over.

'Good to see you,' he smiled, giving me the feeling it was a genuine response. 'I've a nice table for you and your friend over by the window. And the special today is grilled trout with capers and lemon and Spring vegetables in a spinach sauce.'

All the time he was talking, he was expertly steering us over to the table he'd chosen, big enough for two, snugly nestled in a little window alcove overlooking a courtyard. Even at this time of year there was a wealth of green foliage in every corner, almost but not quite hiding the few steps leading up to an old stone wall with a lion's head fountain where a soothing gurgle of water trickled down.

For a few minutes there was silence as we perused the menu. Many of the dishes were strange to me, but I didn't want to reveal my ignorance by asking, so was very relieved when Josie said, 'I'll have an omelette Basque with an undressed salad.'

'Sounds good,' I said eagerly. 'I'll have the same.' After all you can't go too far wrong with eggs though I would have preferred it with chips. Still, it didn't look as if it was that kind of a restaurant.

When Josie had chosen some wine for us (most of which I drank) and some sparkling mineral water (most of which she drank) she sat back in her chair and looked at me with what could only be described as quiet amusement.

Again I was struck by the change in her and wondered idly if she'd had cosmetic surgery. She'd none of the incipient wrinkles people of our age develop. Could someone change as much as she had without help?

She toyed with her glass of mineral water taking small, frequent sips and, with a flash of insight, I suddenly realised she was a nervous as I was. Was that because it had been so long since we'd met? Or was there some other reason that she would reveal over this "friendly" lunch?

'Is this a family visit?' she said.

I hesitated for a moment, but only a moment. There was no point in lying. If I wanted answers, I had to tell her why I'd come to London, but I made it as brief as possible.

She folded her hands on the table and leaned across saying, 'So, Alison, you've decided to rake up the past.'

Well, that's pretty direct I thought, but aloud I said, 'It's not quite like that Josie. I didn't suddenly decide to "rake up" the past. I saw a man who looked like Gabriel Santos on the train from Edinburgh to Glasgow a few weeks before last Christmas. What I mean is, I was sure it was him.' Then aware how confused this sounded, I hurried on, 'and you know as well as anyone that Gabriel died long ago.'

I stopped, daring her to contradict me, or to laugh at me. From the look on her face it appeared my story had taken her completely by surprise, but she made no immediate comment.

In an effort to break the awkward silence I went on, 'It's either my imagination or a legacy of my memory problems because of the car crash.'

Before she could reply, the waiter arrived with our main course and during the pause of a few minutes as he fussed around, a thought struck me. What had she meant by "raking up the past"? What did she really know about the reason for my trip to London?

Under cover of starting on my omelette, I said no more, warily waiting to see what she would do next.

She sat and stared at me thoughtfully, as though weighing up exactly how she should reply. Suddenly she leaned forward, taking me by surprise.

'It's not me you want to talk to, Alison. No, you want to speak to Melanie.' Her voice was bitter. 'Though what Gabriel did to Melanie is really her business and as far as I'm concerned, he should be rotting in hell.'

TWENTY-ONE

Next day I only just managed to catch the one thirty train back to Glasgow. Not that it was really my fault, but Maura had been insistent about ordering a taxi to take me to the station in spite of my protestations about being happy to use the underground. In all my ramblings about the city in the past week, I'd become proud of my proficiency in using the system again. Besides I'd very little luggage, having learned over the years to travel light.

Given the London traffic, the taxi was late, so I arrived at Euston and managed to run onto the train as it was about to leave. The train gathered speed and I made slow progress through the corridors to my seat, trying to keep my balance, apologising to one person after another. Eventually I found the correct carriage and even the right seat, and fell into it gratefully.

Flicking through the various magazines I'd brought didn't take long: the fashion and beauty pages depress me, the home makeover pages remind me our entire house needs a facelift and most of the appetising recipes are beyond me. The problem pages are of passing interest, if only to show what interesting lives some people lead compared to mine.

My mind in turmoil about all that had happened in London, I had a stab at the improving read that had lain untouched in my bag all week, but this year's choice was true to form and my mind began to wander after the first few pages.

The train gathered speed as it headed towards Scotland, and all the problems I'd left there began to loom large.

For one thing, there was the worry about Simon and how to deal with the situation. I'd only spoken to him once and that (deliberately) very briefly. Now I needed time to think, to find out if he was involved in some way with this business.

Not long after Simon and I met I moved out of Kara's into my own flat, so he knew the people there only slightly. And there was now no doubt Josie had some information about Gabriel. It was beginning to look as if I couldn't trust anyone.

In some ways the week away from home had seemed like an eternity and as the miles rolled past I determined to make a plan. After what had happened in London the first action must be to find my diary. It was more important than ever: there must be some clue there, something that would fill in the missing bits in my memory and release me from this continuing vague feeling of dread.

Every so often I took Gabriel's death certificate out of my bag and re-read it, but it made no difference. It was still the same. Gabriel Santos: Cause of death, drowning. There was nothing to give me any real clue. It was all so stark, so final. I folded it and put it back carefully in the middle compartment of my handbag yet again, reflecting on my few days in London. What a lot had happened, none of it as expected.

Josie, for example. I still didn't know whether I should be flattered she'd recognised me after all these years or upset she'd known me. Or was it more than coincidence she'd been in the restaurant that night?

Strange about Kara, too. How your memory plays tricks on you, letting you remember only what suits you. What was the real relationship between her and Gabriel? At the time I accepted he was one of the tenants, but there must have been some reason she let him stay on if she disliked him so much. A dislike she did nothing to hide.

Lunch with Josie had brought so much back that had been buried in my memory, making me realise how naïve I'd been to believe my recovery from the accident had been complete. It was like a gigantic jigsaw where I was slowly but steadily gathering all the pieces, but unfortunately didn't have the picture on the box to help me put them together in the right order.

Not that Josie offered a great deal of help with my quest to find out the truth about Gabriel. After her astonishing statement about Gabriel and Melanie, she had been deliberately vague.

'I'd like to be able to answer all your questions, Alison, but remember I was young myself and didn't really pick up all that was going on. As I've said, the person who could help most is Melanie.'

This was backtracking of a spectacular kind.

'Fine,' I'd said gloomily, 'but how do I now find Melanie?'

This lunchtime meeting wasn't turning out at all as I'd hoped. The omelette wasn't living up to expectations either.

'I've been singularly unsuccessful finding anyone so far. If you hadn't recognised me in the restaurant last night that would have been another missed opportunity. I would certainly never have recognised you.'

For the first time Josie laughed and her whole face lit up.

'I'll take that as a compliment Alison. But we've all changed.'

She paused with her fork halfway to her mouth as though lost in thought.

It didn't escape my notice that while I'd gobbled my lunch down greedily (because I was hungry) she had done no more than toy with the food on her plate and ate very little.

She hesitated for a moment. 'Look, I do want to help you if possible. I'm almost certain I've an address for Melanie somewhere. She went to work in America when it was all over. It's a couple of years out of date but it's a start. Leave it with me,' she said, 'and I'll see what I can do. That is,' she added, 'if you're really determined to pursue this.'

'I've no option, Josie. It's either that or my sanity.'

I hoped this sounded sad enough to dispel any doubts she might have, make her feel sorry for me.

As she pushed her plate away, the waiter came over. 'Everything all right? Would you like a dessert?'

About to say, 'Yes, please,' having spied a trolley groaning with an extensive variety of tempting and calorie- laden goodies, I was forestalled by Josie's, 'No, thanks. We'll have coffee.'

'Oh, sorry, does that suit you, Alison?'

What could I say? 'Fine,' I mumbled, but while Josie opted for a small espresso I ordered a large cappuccino, which fortunately arrived with a handmade chocolate, a consolation of sorts.

It was evident there was no more to be gained from our conversation, unsatisfactory though it was. Everyone seemed to want me to give up my search for the truth, but it was too late for that. Every little scrap of information added to my understanding.

I suspected Josie's resources for finding Melanie were greater than mine and we spent the rest of the time in more relaxed recollections of our time in Hampstead. Once we moved on to safer ground, Josie seemed visibly to soften.

Yet, in spite of the casual friendliness of it all, the impression she knew far more than she was saying kept nagging away at me, not least because of the questions about Gabriel, about my sighting of him that she slipped in to the conversation from time to time.

Sadly, Josie's idea of a long lunch break wasn't mine, and in total we had something like forty minutes together. And I realised how she kept so slim since the restaurant she had chosen served miniscule portions at very expensive prices.

I lay back in my seat and closed my eyes, letting the rhythm of the train lull me into a daydream, drifting slowly off into that half awake, half asleep state when things surface unbidden.

By the time Kara finally came out of hospital I'd found a flat of my own, had begun to enjoy my temping job in a funny kind of way and had met Simon at a party. Being in love is the only way I can explain my lack of concern for what, looking back now, seems a callous disregard for Kara's plight.

She'd been in hospital for much longer than any of us anticipated. Even then the non-stop cheroot smoking had complicated her recovery. In spite of trying hard, I couldn't remember the details about her suicide attempt, if there had been any long-lasting consequences. If she had confided in anyone, it hadn't been me.

Although I visited her in hospital, my assumption was that when she came out the others who lived in the house would take care of her. I was no longer living there and though I did go round from time to time, I didn't always feel comfortable, especially as Gabriel was still living there.

One day, after Kara had been home for a few weeks, he walked back in again as if nothing had happened. Josie had told me that Melanie in her usual blunt way had tackled him about it, but her questions, 'Where have you been Gabriel? Did you not know about Kara's attempt at suicide?' merely elicited, 'Oh, really,' or a shrug of the shoulders. She gave up trying.

No one had any idea why Gabriel kept disappearing like that, only to turn up again when least expected. It wasn't our house, wasn't our concern, but we worried for Kara's sake.

Melanie did pester Kara to take some action, to evict him for good, but she wouldn't, refused to discuss it whenever the subject was mentioned.

After Gabriel returned that last time, she withdrew even more into herself and stayed most of the time in her room. She even gave up going out unless it was absolutely essential. And so the whole atmosphere in the house changed. The relaxed, casual feeling was gone.

Any time I visited there was a tension in the air as though everyone was on edge, waiting for something to happen, and I was glad to escape back to the cosy flat I was sharing with two trainee teachers. Melanie stayed on in Kara's house with Josie and George.

By December George had left and Gabriel was dead.

TWENTY-TWO

The house was unnervingly quiet as I turned the key in the lock calling out, 'Hello, anyone home?'

Complete silence. After waiting for half an hour in a draughty Central Station and being put through to the answering machine when I phoned, I'd decided to make my own way home. It was very puzzling - I'd called Simon from Euston to remind him about the time of the train. Where was he?

Pushing the door closed with my foot, I dumped my case, shivering as I shrugged off my coat in the chilly hallway. 'Simon, are you there? I'm home,' I called out again, suddenly realising he might be in his study listening to music with his headphones on.

No Simon, no note: nothing to indicate where he might be. Guiltily, I remembered my failure to return his last phone message.

There was no sign of Deborah either, though she'd made it clear she'd abandoned her course at Art College; a course of action which would hopefully be temporary.

There was a sound of soft footsteps from the sitting room and Motley came purring over, wrapping himself round my ankles. 'Motley,' I said crossly, 'have you been sleeping in the sitting room?' Of course he made no reply but continued to purr in a most ingratiating manner as I picked him up.

It was hardly his fault if Simon had left the door to the sitting room open, but as Motley is most certainly not allowed in there, I dreaded to think what damage his claws might have inflicted, put him down and closed the door tightly. 'I'll feed you in a minute,' I said.

He followed me as I took my suitcase up to our bedroom where Simon's clothes lay scattered around, though one or two socks had almost made it to the laundry basket. The wardrobe door was wide open as though he'd changed in a hurry to go out: on the other hand it might have been like that for most of the week.

Having hung up my coat, blitzed the worst of the room quickly before having a shower and changing into some less travel-weary clothes, I paused to have a peep into Deborah's room before going back downstairs. It was clear she was still living at home.

The thought of hot food was appealing after a day spent eating sandwiches and in the kitchen, with the central heating now kicking in, I looked in the fridge for inspiration for something quick and tasty, but this revealed no more than a piece of excessively hard cheese, a squashed tomato, a few eggs and some milk. Nothing to tempt the weary traveller there.

Motley came purring round again, looking for food. This was no indication I'd been missed at all, merely that he'd realised his dish was empty and I might be the person who would fill it.

'There's not much here for either of us,' I said, pouring him some milk. He lapped it up without a pause, making me suspect his meals had been somewhat erratic during the past week.

The freezer proved more appealing. I'd left it well stocked before leaving, but evidently Simon had eaten very few of the meals. It was more than likely the local takeaway had done very good business recently, not to mention the pub on the corner. I finally settled on a vegetarian lasagne and popped it in the microwave before going through to the lounge and idly switching on the television.

A short time later, comfortably ensconced on the sofa with my lasagne and a glass of wine, engrossed in a riveting episode of my favourite soap, I heard the sound of the front door opening.

Simon came in to the living room and stopped when he saw me, striking his forehead in horror. 'Oh no, Alison, I forgot all about you.' He looked suitably contrite as he sat down with a thump on the chair opposite me.

'Well, that's a nice welcome home I must say,' was my reply, but it was only half-meant. Guilt about my lack of communication during the week tempered my reproof as he came over to give me a hug.

In spite of my jovial welcome, Simon seemed smitten with remorse. 'How could I have forgotten you were coming home today?' He frowned and ran his fingers through his hair.

'Quite easily it would appear,' I replied, leaning forward and smoothing his hair back into place. 'What happened? Have you been very busy?'

'Give me a minute to get my coat off and I'll explain everything.'

Unable to contain my curiosity, I followed him into the hall, suddenly alarmed by how grim he looked. What on earth had happened?

'Has there been an accident?'

He turned to me as he hung up his coat. 'No, no nothing like that. But it is pretty dreadful. Let's go back through and I'll tell you.'

He went over to the cabinet and poured himself an unusually large measure of whisky, lifting the bottle to ask if I wanted to join him, but I shook my head and he came over to put his free arm round my shoulders. 'Let's sit down.' Another pause. 'I think you'll want to sit down when I tell you.'

There was only one thought in my mind. Was he at last to be truthful with me? Give me answers to some of my questions? Whatever had happened was upsetting him very much. He sat in the chair opposite me and took both my hands in his.

'Alison, I think I'm about to lose my job.'

For a moment bitter disappointment flooded through me and I had this strange desire to laugh, managing at the last minute to turn it into a cough. Whatever I'd expected, it wasn't this. My mind was still full of the problem of Gabriel and anything else seemed of little consequence.

Striving to contain my impatience, I said, 'What on earth do you mean, Simon? I thought all this was sorted out before Christmas and the department had secured funding?'

'So did I, but apparently it's not so certain now. The whole college budget is going to be much less than anticipated next year and there will have to be savings somewhere. The Principal called us all in for an emergency meeting. She's as upset as we are about the situation.'

'And what makes you think that you'll be the one who has to go?'

'Well, they're merging my department with one of the others to cut costs and I'm the oldest member of the new department. I'm too costly to keep.'

'Nonsense,' I said with more bravado than I really felt. 'They'd be mad to want to lose all your experience. I'm sure you're one of the most valued members of staff. And you've only recently been promoted. So how can they do without you?'

'Well, given my age I could be a prime candidate for retirement.'

My heart sank. If Simon was forced into retirement and couldn't find another job, all our careful plans would have to go and even worse, I'd probably have to continue teaching till I was ninety. Putting on a cheerful smile to disguise my dismay, I said, 'Nonsense, I'm sure it'll all work out.' With all this worry about Gabriel and Deborah and now Simon, how would I cope?

It was late when we eventually went up to bed, having exhaustively discussed Simon's (possible) difficulties and resolving not to be upset about them, I'd given him a much-edited version of my week in London with Maura. By then it was almost midnight.

In the circumstances, not wanting to alarm him further, I tried my best to sound upbeat, updating him about Alan and Maura, giving him an edited account of my wanderings around Hampstead. Then, casually, as though it was a throwaway line, I said, 'I did bump into someone I used to know when I lived at Kara's - Josie. Do you remember her?'

There was a fractional hesitation before Simon nodded, turning away so that I couldn't see his face, but he seemed to remember her well.

'A plump girl with that copycat Joan Baez hairstyle, wasn't that her? And those black rimmed glasses everyone wore at the time?'

I looked at him encouragingly, waiting for him to continue, but he didn't appear to notice. Strange, he remembered Josie in such detail but claimed scarcely to remember Gabriel at all. How well did he know her all those years ago? I thought again about the incident in Kara's kitchen when I'd found them together, wondering what he was concealing.

'Not that it matters,' I replied, 'as she's changed out of all recognition.' I paused, looking for some reaction.

Simon, who had a moment before been stifling a yawn, was suddenly fully alert.

'Was she able to help you with this Gabriel business?'

'Not really,' I answered, trying to keep my voice light, casual. 'We had too many girly things to talk about, too many memories of the good times we had at Kara's.'

I tried a suitable giggle but out of the corner of my eye could see Simon regarding me with an odd expression on his face and cut the conversation short. 'Come on, bedtime, I think,' I said.

Simon looked hopeful.

'To sleep,' I said firmly. 'After all, tomorrow is Saturday.'

Then as he yawned again, 'You go on up and I'll do the lights and lock up,' I offered, thinking also to check that Motley was indoors safe and sound. There are too many urban foxes around and I'm sure he's plump enough in spite of his *Weighless Cat Cuisine* to make a tasty meal for them.

At the foot of the stairs I stopped, suddenly wondering if there were any messages on the answering machine apart from mine. There was one message from Susie Littlejohn.

'Alison, don't know if you'll get this to-night or not, but if you're back before 11 o' clock or so, do phone me. I may have some news that'll interest you.'

The clock in the hall said twelve thirty a.m. - too late to phone now. What could Susie possibly have found out? Wondering how to contain my curiosity, I headed for bed and crashed out sooner than expected, not even hearing Deborah return some time in the small hours.

TWENTY-THREE

Saturday was a lost day: by the time we surfaced, both of us in a very fragile state (but for different reasons) it was late morning. And there was still no sign of the diary.

'You should be careful at your age,' Deborah grinned, wagging her finger at me as I came into the kitchen.

'Why don't we go for a walk and blow the cobwebs away?' I suggested later to Simon, but he looked at me as if this was a mad idea.

'I'm better off here for the day, Alison.'

He returned to reading the paper.

I started several tasks, abandoned them all one by one, unable to settle to anything, until finally deciding the day wouldn't be entirely wasted if I paid a visit to my mother. If anything that only made my headache worse.

She was in the middle of some dispute with her best friend and insisted on giving me all the minute details. Fortunately over the years I've learned not to give advice: all she wants is someone to listen.

By evening we were vegetating in front of a succession of inane programmes on the box. Simon was unusually silent, responding with no more than a grunt to my half-hearted attempts at conversation.

In spite of several phone calls I'd no luck in contacting Susie and eventually left a very short message on her answering machine.

Somehow we made it through the weekend and by Monday I was glad of the distraction of the thud of the morning post on the doormat as we went in to the kitchen.

'I'll get it,' said Simon quickly, turning to go back into the hallway.

He seemed to be taking a very long time and I called through, 'Is there a problem?' as I put the coffee on and started to organise some scrambled eggs and toast.

There was no reply and I went on preparing breakfast, wondering what on earth could be detaining him. Just as I was about to investigate, to say, 'Everything's ready,' he appeared in the kitchen. I was making an effort to eat some toast, though the butterflies in my stomach seemed to have other ideas.

He sat down opposite me and took a swig of coffee. 'Something for you, postmarked London,' he said from behind a mouthful of buttered toast. 'The rest seem to be bills, so we can ignore those as we usually do.'

A few months ago, extremely harassed, we each thought the other had paid the telephone bill and it wasn't until we were cut off that we realised that neither of us had. This still rankled with Simon who was usually so punctilious about bills, and he reminded me from time to time, more often than was strictly necessary.

'Thanks,' I said, trying to look unconcerned, although my heart was pounding. I put the letter down on the table as if it were of no consequence, all the while trying to squint at the exact postmark without attracting Simon's attention.

It could only be from Josie. I certainly didn't recognise it as Maura's handwriting or that of anyone else I knew, but for some reason didn't want to open it while Simon was still around. This was something to do on my own, so I went on picking at my breakfast, ignoring the way he kept looking over at me. In spite of his evident curiosity he said nothing and continued eating breakfast, carefully avoiding looking at me directly.

'Do you want a lift?' Simon asked, standing up and swallowing the last mouthful of coffee.

My car was in the garage yet again. It's an old banger that seems to spend more of its life there than on the road.

'No, I've no classes first thing this morning, so there's no need to leave for a while yet. I'll catch the bus.'

He shrugged as I tried to avoid his gaze: being married for as long as we have makes dissembling very difficult. He kissed me on the cheek.

'Suit yourself. Remember I could be a bit late tonight. There's another meeting about this merger and I might go to the pub afterwards with Tony.'

I was about to say, 'Don't overindulge,' but stopped in time. Now was not the moment to be delaying Simon with a reminder about the perils of drink.

As soon as the front door slammed shut, I put down my cup and seized the letter. I was about to tear it open when I noticed there was something odd about the flap of the envelope. It was creased and uneven. I stared at it, fingered it, turned the envelope over, examined it closely. It looked as if the letter had been opened and then reclosed.

Apart from the postman Simon was the only person who'd handled it. Surely the postman wasn't reading our mail?

Tearing open the envelope, I pulled out a single sheet of paper. As expected, the letter was from Josie and she'd been as good as her word. It was coincidence enough she'd managed to contact Melanie, but even better she'd found out Melanie would be in Scotland for a week.

My earlier suspicions of all her talk about "trying to get in touch with Melanie" were confirmed. Of course Josie had known where she was, but probably wasn't too sure Melanie would want to contact me. What were they up to? And what did they know that I didn't? If they'd truly lost touch surely it would have taken her a lot longer than a few days to track down our old friend.

I read and reread the letter, but it was short and to the point, gave no more than the barest details of her success in sorting out a meeting.

In the midst of trying to make sense of this, the phone rang and I dropped the letter among the debris of breakfast, almost tripping over Motley in my haste to reach the kitchen extension.

It was Josie. Her voice was strangely flat.

'Didn't think I'd catch you, Alison, but wanted to let you know I've done my bit if you're still interested in all that stuff from long ago.'

'I've just this minute read your letter,' I said eagerly, 'and I…'

She cut me short.

'I've given Melanie your phone number and she'll be in touch once she arrives in Edinburgh.'

I should have said something then, because I didn't believe her. The laid back, disinterested attitude she'd adopted was surely an act. Of course she knew all about Melanie. What was she trying to hide from me?

She rang off before I could say more than a hurried goodbye, and immediately I ran upstairs to hide the letter at the back of one of the drawers in my filing cabinet. There was no way it was going to suffer the same fate as my diary. There was no more time to think about Josie's call: a glance at the clock told me if I didn't hurry, I'd be seriously late for my first class.

It would have to be a particularly difficult day at school: a departmental meeting straight after break at which we were told how the budgets were to be cut yet again. Simon wasn't the only one who was suffering from the economic downturn.

We all left the meeting more than a little depressed and I had to go straight in to my class of fourth year leavers without so much as a cup of tea. And a cup of tea is the very least you require. None of them wants to be in school and they count the days until their release at the end of term as fervently as any convict. That is when they bother to turn up at all. You never know what kind of mood they'll be in as there are basically only two: total mania or total apathy.

It's hard to know which is worse, but in neither are they interested in anything school provides. As often as not it's a battle of wills to see who can emerge less scarred.

At lunchtime I collapsed into the chair next to Susie at the dining table. Fortunately it was my "off" week for supervision in the dining hall and I could enjoy my meal in peace.

'You look shattered, Alison,' said Susie matter-of-factly as she tucked into her shepherd's pie with gusto. 'Surely you didn't take this morning's meeting too much to heart?'

'Thanks very much for those comments, Susie: that's made me feel a lot better,' I replied with an attempt at sarcasm as I leaned across the table. 'Now, I'm absolutely burning with curiosity. What was that mysterious phone call all about?'

Susie continued, deliberately ignoring my plea, 'It must have been some holiday you had in London. What on earth did you get up to without Simon there?' She grinned, determined to keep me guessing for as long as possible.

'Not as much as you might think unfortunately.' I toyed with my food.

'Not eating, Alison? The food isn't that bad.'

'No, not at all.' I pushed my plate away from me with a sigh. 'Look Susie, either tell me what's going on or let's drop the subject all together.'

'All right,' she grinned wickedly, 'but I must say you're very touchy today. What's bugging you?'

'I'm nervous that's all. I'm meeting up with someone I knew a long time ago, someone who might help me remember what happened then. Trouble is, I'm not sure how it will all go.'

Susie's eyes lit up.

'Oh-ho, I thought so. An illicit relationship is it? Come on Alison; tell Auntie Susie all about it.'

I shook my head.

'No, Susie, I'm afraid you'll have to be disappointed. It's an old flat mate from my time in London - and it isn't even a man.'

Susie pulled her apple tart and custard towards her. She grinned at me.

'What a disappointment you are, Alison. Is there never going to be any excitement in my life?'

'If you want excitement Susie, you'll have to make it for yourself.'

'Come on, Alison, I'm only pulling your leg, trying to cheer you up. I realise you and Simon are an old married couple.'

'I'm not that past it Susie,' I said, bristling a little and then we both collapsed in gales of laughter, much to the curiosity of the others in the dining hall.

Susie was the first to stop, wiping the tears of laughter from her eyes and saying more soberly.

'It may be nothing much, Alison, but while you were away, I thought I'd do some digging of my own. That's what friends are for,' she went on as she saw the astonished look on my face.

'Well, at least that makes me feel a bit better,' I said. 'Now, come on, Susie, what's this all about?'

'Oh, all right. I have my contacts too. Ross knows someone who works at the *Hampstead and Highgate Express*. I'm trying

140

to get some information for you: to find out if there's been any follow-up to that article. If anyone has contacted them about it.'

Was that all?

'Thanks, Susie, let me know if anything comes of your contact. Any information is useful. Don't worry. I'll keep you up to date. Now I must go and prepare for my next class.'

It all sounded very abrupt, but I was in no mood to mull over unlikely possibilities.

The truth was, I didn't think Susie would get anything from her boyfriend's contact. It was all so long ago I doubted if more information, more than had been in the article, would still be on file. The population of West Hampstead was, and still is, so transient, the chances of someone recognising Gabriel, coming up with some earth-shattering news, were negligible. But she was my friend and I had to show some appreciation for the effort she'd made, though that's not how I felt. Susie had raised my hopes by her phone call, but this was another blind alley.

Now my meeting with Melanie was of the utmost importance, a way to find out what she knew about Gabriel's death. She had been the one closest to Kara, had known her best. Then there was that sighting of Melanie in the taxi outside the Theatre Royal. Unless that had also been a figment of my imagination. This was it/wasn't it scenario was becoming unbearable.

In spite of all my concerns, I was so busy in school during the day and so tired from my many sleepless nights there was little time to worry too much about my meeting with Melanie.

Later I discovered I should have been better prepared.

TWENTY-FOUR

For most of the evening I was on tenterhooks, awaiting the promised phone call from Melanie, checking the answering machine every few minutes in case I'd missed her, until finally Deborah said, 'For goodness sake, Mum, come away from there. You're like a cat on hot bricks. There's no way you could miss a phone call.'

Even so, when one of Deborah's friends called after dinner, I insisted Deborah phone her back using her mobile. By the time Melanie did make contact, I was so engrossed in a television programme I'd recorded the shrill ring startled me.

Of necessity our conversation was short. She was phoning from the conference she was attending, and her voice had that mid-Atlantic twang of someone who has spent a lot of time in the States, but she sounded sympathetic, concerned. Perhaps Josie had made her aware of how disturbing the Gabriel business was for me. I had to rely on the fact she'd always been kind to me in those days long past in Hampstead, and would still be willing to help me now.

She said, 'I've a flexible day on Wednesday, Alison, so if that suits you I can make it through to Glasgow and meet you for dinner. Somewhere in town would be best, but you choose.'

'Will I recognise you, Melanie?' I said anxiously, remembering the embarrassment of my meeting with Josie in London.

'Oh, I guess so, though I am older, but then so are you. But to make sure, I'll be wearing a red jacket.'

I didn't necessarily think that would make her stand out in a crowd. I'd better have some distinguishing mark as well so we were both clearly recognisable. No way did I want to be accosting the wrong person the way I'd confronted that poor man in Fraser's.

'And I'll be ...' I racked my brains for something that would fit the bill, but the only thing that came to mind on the spur of the moment sounded mundane. 'I'll be carrying one of those big tote bags with *Born to Shop* on it,' I blurted out.

As one of my less suitable Christmas presents it had been thrown into a cupboard somewhere after the family had made a great joke of it.

'Someone knows you too well,' Simon had laughed.

'In which case I'll never use it,' had been my frosty response. I hadn't looked at it since, so finding it might prove difficult.

Melanie laughed, a rich throaty chuckle that made me hopeful about our meeting.

'And are you, Alison? Born to shop, I mean?'

'Not quite, I don't have that sort of money or leisure time. But I do my best.'

Again she laughed.

'It'll be good to see you, Alison.'

With that she rang off, leaving me gazing thoughtfully at the receiver.

As usual life was so busy it wasn't until the Wednesday morning I suddenly remembered my decision to take the *Born to Shop* bag with me and spent some time rummaging for it, trying first the hall closet, then the cupboard on the upper landing. No sign of it.

'Deborah, did you by any chance borrow that *Born to Shop* bag I was given for Christmas?' I asked her, when yet another search had proved unsuccessful.

'Good heavens, Mum, it's not the kind of bag I'd want to be seen with. Of course, I didn't borrow it.' She sounded indignant at the very idea.

This large garish bag, a present from my second year class, was neither stylish nor useful but it was the kind of bag people would remember. And there was always the possibility if I passed it on to a charity shop one of the second years would spot it.

In a sudden flash of inspiration, I decided to try the top cupboard in our bedroom. It's not often used, because it requires a very dangerous balancing act on the bed, but this was the only place I'd hadn't looked. Perhaps I'd thrown it up there in one of my clearing up bouts of enthusiasm after the Christmas panic had died down.

I stood on tiptoe on the bed, holding on to the cupboard door for support and cautiously pulled it open to ferret about inside. Sure enough, there was something right at the back, only just within reach. Pleased to have found it at last, I tugged it out and was about to drop it beside the window ready for my evening jaunt when I felt something bulky underneath. After a few minutes of ineffective scrabbling about I managed to pull out a brown paper package and sat back down the bed to investigate. Intrigued, I hastily unwrapped the packaging, then stopped, scarcely able to believe my eyes.

Inside the brown paper package was my lost diary.

TWENTY-FIVE

We'd arranged to meet in the little bistro at the top of the Princes Square shopping gallery.

'No, I know where it is,' she replied brusquely when I asked if she needed directions. She had a good knowledge of Glasgow, then? All the more reason to believe she had indeed been the woman I'd seen in the taxi with Gabriel.

Wednesday evening couldn't come quickly enough. Every hour seemed to drag. Even so, there'd been no opportunity to read my diary except for the briefest glance. Simon was working from home for a couple of days, trying to make sense of the departmental budgets and Deborah had come down with a bad cold, so there was no time on my own.

As a temporary measure, I'd stuck the diary at the very back of my underwear drawer, uncertain exactly what to do. It must have been Simon who'd left it in the top cupboard, had moved it from the loft. What I couldn't work out was why he was hiding it from me and, if he did have a good reason for not wanting me to see it, why not destroy it?

One option was to put the bag and the diary back where I'd found it, pretend I hadn't seen it, and think of some other way of letting Melanie recognise me. Or brave it out and take the bag as arranged, hoping Simon wouldn't realise it was missing.

After a lot of thought, I decided on the latter course of action. Surely Melanie would have some information that would help me, set my mind at rest. Besides, if she was still in touch with Gabriel, how could she sound so normal? That still left the puzzle of Josie's comment: "what Gabriel did to Melanie"

It was all too much and I kept going round in circles, unable to find an answer: sometimes convinced I had seen Gabriel, other times certain it had all been a figment of my imagination and somehow I'd had a mental relapse. With every minute that passed I became more and more certain Melanie would have the solution, that the meeting with her would at last give me peace of mind.

By the time school finished at four o'clock I was desperate to head for home as quickly as possible and have a long hot bath in an attempt to relax, before going out to meet her.

I flung the pile of essays on *Hamlet* into the boot of the car. Usually I'd have stayed behind at school to make a start on them, but I'd have to worry about that later, being in no mood to concern myself with Hamlet and his problems: I'd plenty of my own.

What on earth should I wear? A trawl through my wardrobe, hoping for inspiration, provided no answers. After my experience with Josie, determined to make the best impression possible, I eventually settled on a light wool dress, at the last minute adding a coat to ward off the chill of the evening.

Simon seemed to have a lot on his mind these days, making him even more forgetful than usual. The financial situation at the college was still on a knife edge and he was worried about his job, but given what had happened I had this strong suspicion there were other things troubling him, nothing to do with college. How much was to do with me I'd no idea, but if he suspected my mental health was deteriorating, his concern was perfectly understandable. Whatever the cause, it was obvious he had no intention of confiding in me.

We were becoming more and more like strangers, taking every opportunity to avoid each other and when we were together I'd sometimes look up and catch him watching me intently.

Or was this a sign of some kind of paranoia, imagining mistrust where there was none? Hoping to overcome these feelings of doubt, I wrote a quick reminder to Simon about going "to meet a friend", convincing myself it was better to be safe, give him some information.

I emptied the contents of my handbag into the *Born to Shop* tote bag, snapping it shut as I went downstairs.

My choice of the bistro on the top floor at Princes Square proved to be a good one. Midweek, it was the ideal place to have a chat in peace and quiet. We could linger over dinner without feeling guilty about holding up other customers.

On the drive into town to park behind the St Enoch shopping centre it occurred to me I always seemed to be meeting people in restaurants these days, but not really making any progress in finding out the truth about Gabriel.

I reflected gloomily on my meal with Josie, hoping Melanie wouldn't be so abstemious, but this time I was on home territory and a lot more certain of the menu we'd be offered. Besides, I'd be paying for this one.

The King Street Car Park was almost deserted. It's a popular car park for cinema and theatregoers because the charge in the evenings is a flat fee, but to-night there were very few cars. I drew up underneath a street light at the far end, double checking everything was locked up before making my way slowly round to Argyle Street, pausing from time to time to look in the brightly lit shop windows. I was ridiculously early, and while anxious to arrive before Melanie, didn't want to appear too eager.

My nervousness increased on entering the restaurant. All those fear responses hit me: the dry mouth, the thumping heart, but I tried to quell them. This would be my opportunity to find out what had happened in Kara's house in London so long ago, find out if my sighting of Gabriel was real or imagined.

Behave, I told myself sternly. After all, I was the one who'd asked for this meeting with Melanie. Logically there was nothing to fear, but my apprehension was all about the answers she might give me. What she had to tell me might make me feel worse, not better.

In spite of my worries, I recognised her at once. Her hair was short, very short, lighter than I remembered, but close up still had the sheen of red gold I'd so admired when we first met. Besides, there was no mistaking that smile and that fragile air. Beyond any shadow of doubt she was the woman who'd been with Gabriel in the taxi at the Theatre Royal.

Trying to appear calm, I took a deep breath as we exchanged greetings. 'Melanie, good to see you. Did you find the place okay? How are you?' In my nervousness the words tumbled out.

She stood up and, as we hugged, I saw and felt, with a sudden shock, how thin she was, her skin almost transparent, her grey eyes even more huge and luminous than I remembered.

'Not as good as I should be, I guess,' but she smiled warmly at me as she said it.

'Sit down, sit down,' I encouraged her, afraid she would fall over. I was shocked by her appearance; it took me a moment or two to recover. Melanie had never been fat, not even plump, but now it seemed as if you could span her waist with your hands.

'Good to see you,' I said again.

'It's been a long time.'

We both spoke at the same time, and we laughed together, a good way of breaking the ice.

We had no sooner sat down at the table than we were interrupted by the waiter sidling over with the menu. 'This restaurant is fairly quiet, Melanie, so there's no rush. Take your time,' I said.

I couldn't exactly say she was ill, but I was genuinely concerned by her appearance, her thinness and fragility.

There was an awkward pause while I racked my brains for a way to ask the questions I'd rehearsed for days. Somehow they all seemed futile. Where do you begin after all these years? Fortunately Melanie solved the problem by launching straight into the story.

'I'd a letter from Josie, after she phoned, explaining what was bothering you, Alison.'

Her voice was light, slightly breathless, but still with that mid-Atlantic twang I'd noticed on the phone.

'Have you kept in touch with her then?'

This wasn't the first question I'd intended to ask, but seemed the only sensible one.

Melanie shrugged and gave a deep sigh.

'Not really - a Christmas card, the occasional postcard - you know that kind of thing.'

Only too well I thought, remembering all the friends who'd received no more from me over the years. Even worse, speaking to her now made me feel guilty I hadn't kept up with any of the others from Kara's house. Yet why did I suddenly have this insight, this feeling Melanie had no intention of telling me the whole truth, was about to give me a carefully rehearsed story?

Melanie tapped her fingers on the table before she looked at me.

'You know Kara died?'

'Yes, I'd heard that. Was it cancer eventually? She always was a heavy smoker.'

Melanie shrugged. 'Mmm.' She went back to tapping her fingers in a slow and steady rhythm.

'Yes,' I gabbled on, not too coherent in my thinking, 'how awful to rescue her from all that grief and the attempted suicide only to have her die an even more horrible death.'

A strange expression crossed Melanie's face, but before she could speak she broke into a fit of coughing and it was a few moments before she recovered.

'What do you mean by that?'

I poured a glass of water and slid it towards her, but she pushed it away, instead taking a tablet from a box in her handbag and swallowing it.

'Well, it was cancer, wasn't it? All those awful cheroots she used to smoke non-stop.'

There was a pause, the expression on her face impossible to read, her silence an indication she was trying to decide how to reply.

'Melanie, are you ill?' I asked anxiously.

She smiled wryly. 'I suppose you could say that, Alison.' It was clear she wasn't prepared to discuss her health and I leaned across the table towards her. 'What happened, Melanie, in that house of Kara's? What did I miss? What was going on that I didn't understand?' There was urgency in my voice that surprised even me.

The waiter interrupted Melanie's reply, saying, 'Ready to order yet, ladies?'

'Give us a few more minutes,' I said, more crossly than intended and he melted discreetly into the background.

He would be back soon, though. Contrary to my belief, the restaurant was beginning to fill up.

'I suppose we really should choose,' I said, 'then we can talk in peace.'

We applied ourselves to the serious business of selecting from the vast menu and somehow I wasn't too surprised when Melanie opted for the grilled sole with no vegetables while I settled for the crispy chicken with all the accompaniments.

We gave our order quickly, concerned the rapport between us might be broken and it would be almost impossible to regain the same ground. A determination had seized me, something which surprised me, because I'm not usually very assertive, but I couldn't face going away from yet another meeting without an answer. If I was to find my way back to a normal life the only way to do it was to lay Gabriel's ghost once and for all.

'You were saying Melanie,' I gently prompted her, 'that I understood very little of what was going on? I know I was very young, only just out of school, and that was most likely the reason I missed so much.'

'No, Alison,' she corrected me, 'it was you who said that.' For a moment she seemed to be puzzled, then collected her thoughts and went on, 'Yes, there were things happening there. Then and afterwards.'

'To do with Kara?' I prompted again.

'Kara… and others,' was the vague reply.

I saw her thoughts drift away again and tried to keep her on track. There was most certainly something wrong with her, because she wasn't behaving normally.

'Look, Melanie,' I said, leaning forward, 'I'm delighted to see you, for no other reason than because it's good to see you again. But Josie suggested that you might be able to help me. I need to know what happened all those years ago in London and if it's anything to do with me.' There it was - out. There was no option now but to be truthful, tell her the whole story.

Briefly I explained about my sighting of Gabriel, my visit to London and my chance encounter with Josie. I didn't mention the Theatre Royal. If she was being equally honest with me she would surely bring that up without prompting.

'...so to all intents and purposes,' I concluded, 'Gabriel died that summer while we were all living at Kara's.'

Surely now Melanie would tell me I was wrong about Gabriel's death, tell me she was still in contact with him.

Instead she frowned and said, 'There's no doubt that the Gabriel we knew died, drowned in that pond at Hampstead Heath. Kara identified him, remember? And she wasn't likely to make that kind of mistake.'

She paused for a moment and looked intently at me, leaning over to put her hand over mine.

'So you see your sighting of Gabriel was a fantasy, no more than a trick of the light or your subconscious. After all, they say everyone has a double.'

Had I gone to all this trouble for Melanie to tell me everything had been some kind of mistake? If this were true, why had Josie gone to the bother of setting up this contact for me? She could have told me herself.

Consumed now with curiosity, I was more convinced than ever Melanie was being deliberately evasive, that this meeting had been set up, not to give me information, but to persuade me it was all a trick of my imagination and I should forget everything that had happened. I was beginning to feel trapped in some kind of nightmare, to think they were all trying to hide something important from me.

There must be some reason she didn't want me to pursue this. And it didn't explain Josie's comment about what "Gabriel had done to Melanie."

The arrival of the food we'd ordered interrupted our conversation. My mind was in turmoil, but Melanie looked as serene as ever as she picked at her food and we chatted idly about our respective jobs, exchanged current news.

'Not at all,' she laughed when I said how I envied her glamorous life. 'It's not as great as you think doing all this travelling, and one hotel is very much like another.'

She went off into another fit of coughing and it was some time before the spasm subsided.

I could only sit in an embarrassed silence while she recovered, toying with the food, but when the coughing ceased I said, 'Well, in spite of all the psychobabble about my subconscious and tricks of the light, Melanie, there were strange things happening in Kara's house. I can accept I may have been mistaken about seeing Gabriel, but not about the other things. At least you can help me with that. Help me remember and regain my past.'

Surely this direct plea would move her, make her understand how important all of this was to me because until I remembered it all, grasped the past as it really was, I felt adrift, frightened by what was missing from my memory.

She lifted her eyebrows.

'What do you want to know, Alison? I thought you were only interested in whether or not your sighting was really of Gabriel. I've assured you Gabriel Santos died long ago.'

This wasn't a satisfactory answer.

'Could Kara have made a mistake? Or had some reason for covering up?'

Melanie shook her head.

'Forget it, Alison. It wasn't like that.'

After all this time it was difficult to know which were the right questions to ask, but I did know this was an opportunity that might never happen again, so took a deep breath and said, 'Melanie, during that time in the house in Hampstead were you and Gabriel - what I mean is, did you and Gabriel...'

She laughed and finished the sentence for me.

'You mean were Gabriel and I conducting an affair in Kara's house under her nose and upsetting her? No, Alison, not then.'

'It was just, well, the way I saw it Gabriel was making a play for you.' How coy that sounded. Determined to convince her, I scrabbled in my handbag. 'Look I've even brought the evidence,' and I pulled out my photograph of that sunlit day on Primrose Hill to pass it over to her.

'Now you can't tell me Gabriel isn't looking at you with more than passing interest in that photograph, Melanie.'

She put down her knife and fork and shook her head sorrowfully, although she was smiling as she looked at the photograph.

Now I was annoyed, cross at all this sidestepping of the truth about Gabriel.

'What's so funny, Melanie?'

For a moment it appeared she wasn't going to reply, but suddenly she lifted her head from the photo and smiled again at me.

'Oh, Alison, Alison, how little you knew. How little you know now. It wasn't me, or Kara that Gabriel was interested in then. No, the person that Gabriel was having a relationship with was George.'

TWENTY-SIX

Time seemed to have stopped as I sat there, my fork poised in mid air, opening and closing my mouth like a goldfish.

Gabriel and George was the last thing I'd have thought of: it was more likely he was having a relationship with Melanie and this was a way of putting me off.

She seemed amused at the look on my face because she said with a smile, 'Don't be so alarmed, Alison. You must have had some idea?'

Still trying to digest this news, I put my fork down and attempted to speak, but nothing would come out. Eventually after a couple of attempts I managed to say, 'I honestly had had no suspicion at all. It didn't occur to me. Are you certain?'

A closer examination of the photograph reassured me: it appeared no different from before. It was Melanie who'd made a mistake or else she was trying to deceive me for some reason known only to herself, trying to throw me off the scent.

'Are you sure?' I repeated. There was no way I could now tell her about my sighting at the Theatre Royal before Christmas. It was difficult enough to find a form of words to move this conversation forward, and now Melanie looked bored.

She toyed again with the food on her plate before replying, 'Alison, even you must have realised that there was something out of the ordinary going on in that house of Kara's. I know you were very young and very naive but it was obvious to everyone.'

She wasn't going to put me off quite so easily and I bristled at her description of me. What made her think it was obvious to everyone? It certainly hadn't been evident to me.

There was an edge to my voice as I replied, 'Well, Melanie, my distinct impression is that Gabriel was pretty fixated on you: even if you didn't return his feelings. Actually I've seen you with him - and recently.' There, I'd said it, even if my description of the occasion was vague. I pretended to look away, all the while stealing a sidelong glance at her, making an effort to eat the last bit of chicken on my plate, trying to judge her reaction.

Now she was almost scornful.

'What you thought was happening and what was actually happening were two quite different things, Alison.'

This was nonsense, all this pussyfooting round the real questions. She didn't she want to admit to a relationship with Gabriel, or that they were still in contact.

No matter what she said, I couldn't get that picture of her and Gabriel in Kara's kitchen out of my mind, the way he lingered beside her, the air between them charged with a current that seemed electric. That wasn't my imagination: it had happened.

A deep breath and then I said, 'If Gabriel is dead and this whole thing has been a figment of my imagination, then surely you can tell me what went on. I honestly can't believe that there was nothing at all between you two.'

She gazed at me, coolly appraising, deciding what exactly she should say.

'All that was later, Alison, much later. That much you have to believe.'

'And George, what happened to George?'

Her eyes narrowed.

'Oh, George is still around. The last I heard - many years ago, mind you - he had moved to Glasgow to work for Brendlands. They took over that firm in London he worked for.'

'George moved to Glasgow?'

I was astonished. It was hard to believe George been so close all this time.

There was a moment's silence, as though she regretted giving me even this sliver of information. 'Not that it matters. It's more than likely he's moved on again somewhere. As I said, it was all some time ago.' She slid up her sleeve and looked at her watch. Once more I noticed how thin her wrist was.

'I'll have to go, Alison, I'm due at the Marriott hotel in about half an hour to meet some clients and I can't be late.'

She stood up abruptly and made to take her purse out of her handbag.

'No, no, Melanie, I'm going to pay for this.' Then I had a brainwave. 'You can pay for the next one.'

She shrugged. 'If you like.' Then quickly, 'It may be a long time until the next one though.'

I wanted to detain her, to find out more, but couldn't think what to say. No one seemed interested in helping me, not really. What they all had in common was a desire to persuade me to forget everything, forget that time in London, make me think I was making a mistake about seeing Gabriel. No one appeared to understand the only piece of information I wanted was to know for sure Gabriel was dead, that I was well and my memory fine. Then I could pick up the pieces of my life again.

What concerned me most was that both she and Josie had given every appearance of wanting to help, but in the end what they had to tell me amounted to very little. They wanted me to believe Gabriel had died all those years ago, but neither was willing to give me any real proof. In fact, it seemed as though they were more interested in finding out what I remembered about those years in London.

Whatever had happened Kara's house had lain dormant for many years and now I wanted the truth. Seeing Gabriel on that train from Edinburgh had brought everything back, all those events in Kara's house. It was as though I'd had a glimpse of the past, my past, and was no longer in control and I didn't like that one little bit. Until my memory was fully restored, I would never settle, never be happy again.

Quite abruptly, Melanie leaned over and kissed me lightly on the cheek, for all the world as if this had been no more than two old friends meeting for a regular meal. Again I felt her thinness; her almost ethereal lightness and her kiss was like the touch of a feather on my skin: she was either anorexic or else very ill.

'Keep in touch, Alison. Give me a ring sometime.'

Still upset our meeting had taken me no further forward, except for the very dubious suggestion of a relationship between Gabriel and George, I couldn't think of a suitable reply.

It appeared she'd no intention of meeting me again while she was in Scotland, so this was some kind of a game was she playing. Or was she trying to pacify me, persuade me to drop my investigation?

'Good luck, Alison. Get on with your life. There's no point in dwelling on the past. It's over, done with.'

With that she was gone, with a swift click of heels on the highly polished floor.

I sat there looking after her, gazing into space, trying to take in what she'd said until the waiter came hovering at my elbow for the third time.

'Are you sure there's nothing else I can get for you?'

It would have been prudent to order another coffee, but instead I opted for a large glass of red wine, hoping it would help me gather my thoughts. I'd collect the car first thing in the morning.

Determined to make some sense of our meeting, I pulled a paper napkin over and took a pen from my bag thinking perhaps if I wrote down everything I could remember of what Melanie had said straight away, then I might be able to come to some conclusion. But after scribbling a few words I soon realised this would be no help at all, as there was precious little to write.

Melanie was being deliberately evasive. After all this time, all the sleepless nights, there were still no answers to my questions.

What a waste it had all been: the visit to London, the meeting with Josie, this dinner with Melanie. None of these had taken me any further forward in finding out the truth.

But being stubborn by nature I couldn't let it go, finish everything there. Melanie's attempts to put me off had made me even more determined to find out what she and Josie were hiding. It was my sanity at stake, and I wasn't prepared to compromise on that.

Melanie knew the truth: the whole truth. She'd been less than convincing about Gabriel being dead. If he was still alive, who had drowned in that pond on Hampstead Heath? And who was the person with Melanie at the Theatre Royal, unless Gabriel had a double?

Now I was cross with myself for leaving so much unsaid, for wasting this opportunity. I could have asked her outright about that evening at the Theatre Royal, demanded an explanation.

She must have known why Gabriel had gone to Paris during the time he was living at Kara's, must have had some idea about the reason for Kara's suicide attempt, if indeed that's what it was.

The waiter returned with the wine and I scarcely registered drinking it, suddenly noticing in surprise that the glass was empty.

On the train home I went over everything that had happened again and again, chiding myself for becoming involved in all this in the first place.

Melanie was right. I had been aware that there was something going on in Kara's house, but I'd been young, more concerned with my own problems and my own life, with no time and even less inclination to start worrying about what was happening to other people.

Nothing had changed. There was more than enough to think about in my life at the moment, between Deborah's crisis about her future and what was happening to Simon and his job. Yet I had to persist.

Then, with a sudden flash of insight, I realised that they all had one thing in common. Simon, Josie and now Melanie were all trying to persuade me to drop my pursuit of Gabriel or his ghost.

The problem was the exact opposite to what I thought. I'd been trailing all these people from the past, trying to find out what had happened, find out whether I was having some kind of breakdown.

But in fact, they thought that I knew something, something important that they most certainly didn't want me to remember. In spite of their apparent willingness to help me, I now had this awful feeling of being no more than a pawn in some game they were playing. Only they knew the rules.

If Melanie hadn't let slip that George had relocated to Glasgow, I wouldn't have bothered doing anything else. I'd have given it up, persuaded myself that it was better to let sleeping dogs lie, tried to put it all behind me.

That was her big mistake. It seemed like fate that he was here in the same city. There would surely be no harm in my renewing my acquaintance with him.

I thought about my diary, still carefully hidden in the chest of drawers. I had to spend time reading it. There must be a clue of some kind there.

Once I'd discovered what it was, armed with the right information, I'd be able to face George.

This time I'd be sure to ask the right questions.

TWENTY-SEVEN

Simon had been assured a decision would be made by the end of the week about his department, but the deadline came and went with no whisper of what was to happen, whether his job was safe.

There was a lingering tension in the air. If I asked how the college funding bid was progressing, his reply was abrupt. Yet if I didn't ask, I'd be unfeeling and uncaring. It was a no win situation.

'What do you know about it, Alison?' or, 'It's all right for you, working in a school. A college is a completely different world,' was his stock response.

Several times in the course of these conversations, I was about to complain that a college department, in spite of all its problems, wasn't the same as a school in a large Glasgow housing scheme. Instead, with commendable restraint, I said as little as possible, preferring to believe his bad humour wasn't only down to concerns about his job. Having the distraction of thinking about making contact with George gave me a focus, helped me cope with the problems at home.

The following Saturday, as soon as Simon left to play golf with his colleague Tony, I went upstairs to examine the diary more carefully. Simon had made no mention of it, showed neither emotion nor any sign he knew it was no longer where he'd left it, in spite of my attempts to drop hints about "reminders of the past."

Comfortably settled on a chair in the kitchen, a large cup of coffee beside me, I opened it up. That was odd. It seemed to be thinner than when I'd first found it in the attic. Some of the early entries were scrappy, no more than a date and a few scribbled lines. Back then I was probably too busy enjoying life to devote much time to writing about it.

The first few pages were all about my journey to London by the overnight bus from Buchanan Street in Glasgow to Victoria Coach Station - a journey not for the faint hearted, though it had the advantage of being cheap.

There were descriptions of all the people in the house when I arrived: Josie, Melanie, George and Kara. I'd forgotten how good looking George was and began smiling to myself as I read on, reliving forgotten stories of our happy times in that house in Hampstead.

At this distance, it was intriguing to see how small my universe had been: the diary was all about me and my relationships, though a visit to *BIBA* did merit a page all to itself, another sign of my shallowness.

With increasing certainty I realised there was a bigger problem than my neglect of the wider world. Quite suddenly the diary came to a halt at the very point when Gabriel returned to Kara's house. I flicked backwards and forwards. There was no mistake: all the pages to do with Gabriel had been very carefully cut out. The diary finished with his return.

Defeated, I sat back and stared at the spaces where the entries should have been. It was perfectly possible I'd disposed of these pages. I'd no recollection of keeping a diary at that time, so possibly disturbed, upset about something, I'd tried to get rid of the incriminating pages. Or had they had been taken out by someone else? The only possible culprit was Simon. Why on earth would he do that?

Then a terrible idea came to me. Simon thought I had some information, something about Gabriel, something he didn't want me to remember. It was the only explanation for this strange behaviour. If that was the case, why not get rid of the diary altogether?

Another dead end. More than ever my hope of finding out the truth rested with George. Any doubts I had about contacting George now vanished.

*

Brendlands Independent Computer Services Limited is now one of the biggest firms in the UK, big enough to have several Scottish offices and according to Melanie, George was working in the Glasgow branch.

My first problem was a great difficulty in remembering George's surname. I must have known it at some time, must have been introduced to him by his full name but it was all so casual at Kara's it had slipped my memory. Thank goodness there was some part of the diary left and I thumbed quickly back through the early pages. Yes, there it was: George King, that was his name.

The telephone isn't my favourite means of communication, something to do with all those disembodied voices, but I summoned up my courage and dialled the number for the Glasgow office listed in the phone book.

'Could I speak to George King, please?'

The clipped voice on the other end said, 'Which department?'

'I'm not sure,' I mumbled, beginning to think this had been a bad idea. 'He may have moved recently.'

'Just a moment, caller.'

There was a whirring and several clicks and then the sound of some raucous music. I held the receiver away from my ear.

'Could I, may I, speak to Mr King?' I blurted out, when a female voice finally answered.

'Who's calling please?'

'Alison Cameron, no, Alison Graham. He'll know me better by that name.'

'I'll check if he's available.'

More raucous music until at last she came back on the line.

'I'm afraid he's not here at the moment. Can I ask him to call you back or can I take a message?'

She sounded bored, disinterested. The cowardly bit of me wanted to hang up, forget it all.

If I didn't, I'd have to think of a suitable message to leave for him. 'Well, George I know I haven't spoken to you in goodness knows how many years but is there any truth in the rumour that you and Gabriel were having an affair? Is it true that Gabriel Santos isn't dead, but still alive?'

I didn't think so, somehow: it was impossible to summarise all those years in a few words.

The voice on the other end of the phone was now sounding impatient.

'Hello, caller. Is there a message you would like to leave for him?'

My reply came out in a rush, 'Could you tell him I phoned and if he could possibly contact me?'

I left my number and put the phone down with a mixture of frustration and disappointment, knowing there was nothing else to do except wait and hope George would return my call soon.

Doubts began to assail me. What if he didn't remember me? What if he wondered why I should be contacting him after all this time without so much as a Christmas card in the intervening years? Or dismissed me as a crank and ignored my message?

An even worse thought struck me. What if all this was some kind of conspiracy everyone except me knew about?

I should have been more explicit, tried to convey the importance, the urgency of it all, but it was too late now. I had to hope that George would be sufficiently intrigued by my call to respond.

There was nothing else I could do for the moment and Simon would be home soon. I went into the kitchen to start the evening meal, dithering even more than usual about what we should eat. The last thing on my mind was food, but somehow I pulled the ingredients together.

The vegetables were simmering on the stove when I heard Simon coming in, and as I glanced up at the kitchen clock my heart sank. He was home early, so it must be bad news.

I took a deep breath and went into the hall, wondering what sort of mood he'd be in, how we would weather yet another storm. But there was no need to say anything. Simon was grinning from ear to ear.

'We've done it, Alison,' he cried lifting me off my feet and twirling me round, something he hadn't done for years when I was a good stone (or more) lighter. 'The funding's been agreed.'

'Simon, put me down.'

I was breathless and giddy. He did as requested and hugged me tightly instead.

'Isn't it great, Alison?'

He looked ten years younger.

'Brilliant, Simon, when did you hear?'

In spite of my concerns I couldn't be other than pleased at this good news. We linked arms and wandered through to the living room.

'At lunchtime,' he said, 'and of course no one could concentrate after that.'

'I'd guessed that,' I said dryly. 'Have you been in the pub all afternoon?'

He refused to rise to the bait. 'Not quite, we had eventually to go back to the department, but I did send everyone home early. Including me.' He laughed uproariously at his own wit.

'Are you hungry, will I put the rest of the meal on now?'

'Never mind all that. Give me a kiss.'

I kissed him briefly. Delighted as I was for him, this euphoria was hard to take after weeks of his suspected deception.

He hugged me again.

'Tell you what. Let's go out to eat. A celebration to show I've appreciated your support during this ghastly business. It's the least I can do. I must have been very difficult to live with.'

About to protest that the meal was almost ready, I said instead, 'Absolutely fine. Dinner can go into the fridge and will save me thinking about a meal for tomorrow.' Then I added, 'On one condition - that you let me drive.'

For once he didn't disagree.

We didn't go far, only to the local Italian restaurant, where you can rely on the food to be well priced and tasty, but Simon did consume a fair amount of wine with the meal as he outlined his plans for developing the department.

Having had a fairly substantial school lunch, I was hard pressed to do justice to another large meal, though I did my best. At this rate, I'd have to join Motley on his *Weighless Cat Cuisine* diet for a few weeks.

The journey home was short, but by the time we reached the house he'd nodded off and I had to waken him. 'Thank goodness tomorrow's Saturday,' I said, pointing him in the direction of the stairs and bed.

'Aren't you coming up?' he said plaintively.

'In a minute,' I said. 'You go ahead.'

'I do feel a bit tired,' he said with a yawn.

I'd done a great job during the evening of pretending all was normal: now I wanted some time to myself.

In the hall the red eye of the answering machine winked at me rhythmically. Before checking it, I went into the living room and switched on the fire, and then went back and listened at the foot of the stairs for the sound of Simon's snoring.

The only reason for Simon's strange behaviour was worry about me. He was concerned that awakening old memories would cause me to have a serious mental relapse. I didn't dare think of any other possibility.

Even so, I put the volume on low before listening to the message. It was terribly crackly and faint as though the speaker was a million miles away and I had to replay it several times before it made sense.

It was George, returning my call, saying he was pleased to hear from me after all this time and suggesting we meet up at his place on Sunday.

Rather taken aback by this positive reply, I hesitated about taking up his offer, but convinced myself there could be no harm in going over to see him, especially as the address he gave me was a respectable part of Hyndland in the west end of Glasgow.

After listening to the message again, I noted the details down in my pocket diary before erasing it. No sense in causing any more complications than necessary.

Now I'd have to think of another reason for going out on Sunday to meet up with George, one that didn't sound too suspicious although it was difficult at the moment to think of anything.

Upstairs I slid into bed, knowing there was no possibility of falling asleep immediately and gave Simon a sharp dig in the ribs to stop him snoring. If I wasn't sleepy, his snoring certainly wouldn't help.

There in the dark, listening to his steady breathing, debating whether to get up and read for a while till I felt sleepy, a million possibilities about the sequence of events so far whirled round in my head.

I went over and over all that had happened since I'd seen Gabriel on the train from Edinburgh, all the missed opportunities to find out the truth. This time I'd insist on some answers from George. Then, armed with some real information, I'd confront Simon.

TWENTY-EIGHT

Simon wasn't quite as perky the next morning. He sat at the table in the kitchen nursing his coffee and staring at the morning paper.

'You've been looking at that same page for the past half hour,' I reminded him. 'Don't you think you should go back to bed for a while?'

He shook his head. 'I'll feel even worse if I do that,' he said. 'Unless of course you're offering to keep me company?'

'Wishful thinking at the moment?'

This at least made him smile.

I poured more coffee and as I busied myself clearing up, he suddenly said, 'How did your meeting go with Melanie?'

'My meeting with Melanie? How did you know about that?'

He looked up.

'Why, you told me.'

'No, I'm sure I didn't say I was meeting Melanie,' I said, stressing the name.

'You must be mistaken, Alison, I'm sure you said that you were meeting her for a meal to try to find out more about this business of Gabriel.'

I was absolutely certain all I'd said to Simon was that I was meeting a friend, so how did he know? Or was this yet another sign that my memory was playing tricks on me? Had I told him and then forgotten? A little shiver of fear went through me. Best not to prolong the conversation.

'Oh, it was very pleasant, a chance to have a chat about the old days, but not very informative...' I improvised.

'So she wasn't able to tell you much more about Gabriel and his death?'

'Nothing really: she didn't seem to know much.'

'Have you arranged to meet up again?'

'Unlikely, it was only a bit of luck that she was in Glasgow for a conference and had some time to spare.'

Was it my imagination again, or did I detect something like a look of relief flicker momentarily across Simon's face?

'I'll put on some fresh coffee,' I said brightly, in an attempt to change the subject.

Simon got to his feet.

'No thanks, not for me. I'll get dressed and go for a walk down to the park. That should clear my head.'

'Good,' I said firmly. 'Remember you promised we could go over to the shopping centre today to look for some new furniture.'

He groaned.

'Oh, must we? I don't feel in the mood for fighting through the Saturday traffic to join the hordes of shoppers.'

'Yes, Simon, if you remember we were going to do this before Christmas but you were worried about spending money if you were about to be made redundant. However, now that your job is secure for a further three years at least...' I left the sentence unfinished but he got my drift because he sighed audibly and made for the stairs.

As he went upstairs, Deborah was coming down. I looked at the kitchen clock.

'Don't worry, Mum, that is the right time. I'm up early because I'm going into town with Stacy. She's trying to find an outfit for her aunt's wedding.'

She grabbed a piece of cold toast as she opened the fridge to pull out a carton of orange juice.

'That's not much of a breakfast to set you up for a day of shopping,' I teased.

She waved the piece of toast around airily. 'Don't fuss: we'll have lunch in town.' With that she was gone.

As I was finishing clearing up the kitchen, Motley came purring round and I poured him some milk, though he indicated he was after something more substantial.

'Later,' I said firmly as he sniffed the milk disdainfully.

He strolled off with his nose in the air in that way cats have of making you feel really mean, but I was determined not to overfeed him. 'It's all for your own good,' I called after him.

'All for whose own good?' asked Simon reappearing in the kitchen fully dressed, including his coat.

'Oh, I was talking to Motley.'

He grinned, 'First signs, Alison...'

'Don't be too long, if we want to beat the traffic,' I reminded him.

'I'll have a brisk walk to the park and back. You can time me if you like.'

He gave me a quick peck on the cheek and went out, slamming the front door noisily behind him.

No sooner was he gone than I remembered we were almost out of milk: he could collect some from the corner shop.

'Drat,' I said and went to the front door. If I hurried I could catch up with him, so I put the front door on the latch and ran down to the bottom of the path, but there was no sign of him.

You must be walking quickly, I thought, but as I turned to go back indoors I suddenly caught spied him at the bottom of the street, heading in the other direction.

Wherever he was going, it wasn't to the park. I hesitated, but only for a moment. After our earlier conversation about Melanie, not to mention all the blind alleys I had been led up by other people, there had to be some reason he'd told me he was setting off for the park and then decided to walk in the opposite direction.

The way he had turned, to the left, led to the station and I didn't think he was planning to run away. A trip to the shopping centre to look at furniture wasn't his favourite pastime, but it surely wasn't enough to make him try to escape.

I ran back indoors, grabbed my bag from the hall table and closed the front door behind me, only then remembering to check my front door key was in it. Fortunately it was.

My heart was pounding. Trying to follow someone and not be seen was a new experience for me, and it wasn't anything like as easy as it appeared in so many detective films. I kept as close as was practical to the gardens of the neighbouring houses, wondering what sort of excuse I could give if caught. Cautiously I crept round the corner and the station came into view. No sign of Simon anywhere.

At the ticket office beside the entrance there was still no Simon, merely a pair of very bored teenagers fooling about. The woman in the ticket office was regarding me strangely and I gave her a reassuring wave, but she continued to stare as I dived out of sight.

Unable to guess where Simon might be, baffled by this turn of events, I turned to leave. As I walked back in the direction of the house, there he was in the phone kiosk, talking animatedly into the handset. Fortunately his back was towards me.

For a moment I couldn't move. There was no reason for him to make a call from a public phone box rather than from the landline, or even his mobile. Whatever his reason, I had to get away as quickly as possible before he spotted me, and took to my heels, arriving back at the house a few minutes later very out of breath.

I'd only managed to take my coat off and settle with the paper, trying to give every impression of having been here since he left, when I heard the front door open and Simon came through.

'Did you have a good walk?' I said, putting the paper to one side.

'Well, it cleared the cobwebs.'

'And was the park busy?'

Surely now he would say he'd changed his mind about the direction of his walk, that there was some simple explanation for his being in the public phone box?

Instead he said brightly, 'No, only a few parents with toddlers keen to feed the ducks.'

I said nothing, waited for him to tell me more, admit he'd been to the station. But he turned and left the room without another word.

Why was he lying and what had he been up to?

TWENTY-NINE

Try as I might, it was almost impossible to come up with an excuse for my visit to George, especially as Simon's unexplained call from the public phone box made me very wary indeed of telling him anything.

All day Saturday I'd kept watch, but at no stage did he give an indication there was anything amiss. We made our way round various furniture stores, had a very pleasant lunch in one of the in-store cafes, but nothing was said. He even seemed more cheerful than usual, given his views on shopping. In the end we didn't agree on new furniture though we whittled down the choice to a possible three sofas, but keeping up this pretence all was normal was exhausting me.

Most Sundays we're at home chilling out with the papers for the afternoon before walking along the road to our local pub for a pre-dinner drink. This Sunday I'd have to think of an excuse to change my routine.

Inventing a family crisis would only make things worse. Finally I came up with the idea of saying I was going shopping. There was no way he would want to come along with me, and even I only attempt to look for a new outfit at the weekend out of dire necessity.

'Simon, you remember we're going to Susie's party next Saturday?'

'Yes, I remember.' He didn't sound too enthusiastic. 'What's the name of this chap she's involved with now?'

'It's Ross,' I told him for the umpteenth time.

'Don't sound so cross, Alison. How am I expected to remember all the details about Susie's love life?'

Simon made it sound as if Susie had a different lover every week, whereas she and Ross had been together now for almost a year.

'Well,' I went on hurriedly, 'the trouble is I've nothing to wear. I thought I'd try to find something this afternoon. I won't be long.'

'Are you going to trail all the way into town on a Sunday? You know what the parking's like and there's no way I'm becoming involved with all those maniacs who only venture out on a Sunday. It was bad enough yesterday.'

'Not at all. I thought I'd pop down to that new little boutique in Hyndland (that at least placed me in the right locality for George). I hear they have some really good stuff and are pretty cheap.'

The last bit added before he could make comments about designer clothes and the cost after the expense of Christmas.

Simon sighed.

'If you can be bothered, but as far as I can see you've a whole wardrobe of clothes upstairs.'

'Yes, but nothing suitable,' I said, in a way that brooked no further argument.

I felt pretty pleased with this subterfuge and did have every intention of calling into the boutique. All I'd done was omit to mention that I was going to see George, but a few moments later panic struck me. Concerned about finding an excuse to go over to Hyndland, I'd given no thought about what might happen once there.

It would be a good idea to tell someone about my plans and for a brief moment I considered Deborah, but as quickly decided this wasn't possible without going through the whole story. There was no point in phoning Maura in London. Alastair I didn't even consider. His memory is so atrocious

176

he'd be quite likely to phone Simon to ask, 'Where was it Mum said she was going and I hadn't to mention?'

Susie sprang to mind. She was the obvious person. There'd be no need to spend time filling her in with the story or trying to make up an excuse since she knew, at least in part, about my concerns.

Trying hard to make little noise, I lifted the extension in the bedroom and dialled her number. Please let her be at home, I thought, crossing my fingers for additional good luck. For once she was.

'Goodness, Alison, I didn't expect to hear from you today. Is there a problem?'

'No, or I hope not,' I replied, speaking closely to the receiver.

'Alison, I can hardly hear you. There seems to be a bad connection.'

'There's nothing wrong with the connection, Susie,' I hissed. 'I don't want Simon to overhear. I need your help urgently.'

'Good gracious, what are you up to now, Alison,' she said almost crossly.

In no mood for games, I said, 'No, listen, Susie, this is really important,' and proceeded to give her brief details of my meeting with George together with instructions about what to do if I didn't return by five o'clock.

'But Alison,' Susie protested not unreasonably, after listening to my story, 'how will I know if you don't come home by then?'

Mmm - that was a difficulty.

'I expect to be back by then at the very latest, so if you ring to speak to me on some pretext or other then I should be at home.'

'Yes, if that will help you.' She sounded doubtful. 'Are you sure you don't want me to come with you, or wait outside the flat?'

'I wouldn't dream of it, Susie,' I said. 'This is a purely precautionary measure. I'm sure it'll all be fine. Speak to you later.'

As I went to ring off before she had the chance to make any further suggestions, I heard a click, as if the extension handset in the kitchen was being replaced, but dismissed it as no more than my overactive imagination at work again.

By this time I was running late, so instead of having time to sort through my wardrobe and find something smart but not too formal, I had to put on my stand-by navy trouser suit - not quite the image I'd hoped to project.

'Bye, Simon, won't be too long,' I called into the kitchen where he seemed to be happily ensconced at the table with a pot of coffee and a pile of newspapers and slipped out of the front door before there was any opportunity for discussion.

The Sunday traffic was still light so yet again I was far too early and drove along Great Western Road towards the West End as slowly as possible, even taking the long way round by Byres Road, steadfastly ignoring the impatient drivers tooting at my lack of speed.

It wasn't difficult to find the Victorian tenement in Novar Drive where George lived. Tenements in Glasgow are broadly divided into two kinds: those with upmarket tiled "wally" closes and those that are merely painted. This one was very upmarket indeed, the polished green and dark brown embossed tiles showing years of careful preservation.

A stout door of solid oak barred my way and I peered at the list of names on the entry phone system by the door. All were on tiny elegant brass plates ranging from the plain and simple to imitation Rennie Macintosh.

I finally found George's name on one of the unadorned plates and rang the doorbell, hearing it echo hollowly down the close, far inside. There was a moment's pause.

'Hello?' The voice on the other side of the entry phone was muffled, indistinct.

'It's Alison, Alison Cameron, I mean Graham,' I replied speaking close to the machine.

'Come on up.' The voice still sounded muffled.

The buzzer sounded and the door yielded to my push surprisingly lightly to allow me to enter the long tiled communal close leading to all the flats.

Once inside, I closed the heavy door behind me and stopped for a moment, trying to collect my thoughts, rehearse exactly what to say.

The stairs were steep and winding and I pitied the flat dwellers having to climb them many times a day. On the third floor I hesitated again, breathlessly, peering at the names on the two doors on that landing. Only one of the stair lights seemed to be working, the others either broken or switched off.

As I was trying to make out the names, the door to the flat on the right suddenly opened and a voice said, 'Come in, Alison, come in.'

There was no way back now. Unlike my encounter with both Josie and Melanie, I'd given a lot of thought to my questions for George, determined not to give up until I had some real answers.

Even so, my heart was pounding and my feet felt as if they were made of lead as, struggling to put one foot in front of the other, I went forward into the dimness of the flat through the wide open door.

Standing in the hallway, illuminated by the soft glow of a single table lamp, was Gabriel Santos.

THIRTY

Gabriel smiled in that sly way I recalled so well, his teeth reminding me of a shark in the half light.

'Alison, you look as if you've seen a ghost.'

His voice was soft and seductive, exactly as I remembered. He was a bit greyer, with a few lines hardly noticeable in the dimness of the hallway, but it was most surely Gabriel.

An icy shiver ran down my spine. My inclination was to turn and run away from here as fast as possible, but I couldn't move, couldn't speak. Of all the scenarios I'd envisaged, this certainly wasn't one of them.

But now it had happened, now Gabriel stood there, very much alive, it seemed the most natural explanation in the world for all that had gone before. What it didn't explain was what had become of George.

It was too late. Even had I been able to move, there was no escape as Gabriel had quietly, but firmly, closed the inner door behind me.

'Come through, Alison, let's have a drink. We'll be more comfortable in the sitting room.'

That same slow soft voice, mesmerising me.

I'd only be comfortable completely away from here, away from this malevolent presence, but as though in some kind of nightmare, I allowed him to take me by the hand and lead me through to the room at the front of the flat, wishing fervently my knees would stop their involuntary knocking.

What on earth had I done? This was much worse than my very worst guess, my very worst imaginings.

The only crumb of consolation was at last I knew there had been no mistake. Here was the man on that train from Edinburgh to Glasgow, the same distinguished profile, the same look. It was the Gabriel Santos I'd recognised that day in November. I hadn't imagined it, I wasn't mad.

In spite of the awful circumstances of being imprisoned here with Gabriel, a little bit of me rejoiced. There was nothing wrong with my mind, in spite of what everyone had done to convince me otherwise. I didn't have any trauma as Susie had suggested, I hadn't been seeing things as Simon thought. I was quite sane. Gabriel wasn't dead: he was living and breathing.

He motioned me to sit on one of the two matching pale cream sofas on either side of the large wrought iron fireplace. I sat down carefully on the edge, all the while keeping my eyes firmly fixed on the Chinese rug that covered the stripped pine floorboards, consoling myself that in the soft muted lighting he wouldn't be able to see my terror.

He fussed around, straightening the cushions at my back, making me jump, taking a ghoulish pleasure in my discomfort.

For a fleeting moment I wondered if he planned to murder me and then a ridiculous thought struck me. If he did, there was no way he could get my body down all those stairs without being seen. This wild speculation was suddenly interrupted by his question.

'White wine all right for you, Alison? I don't think it's wise to drink anything too strong in the afternoons. But a glass of well chilled Chablis is, I think, most acceptable.'

I stared at him. How could he be chatting in this way as though we were no more than two old friends sharing a pleasant Sunday afternoon drink together?

Best to humour him, not make him angry and I tried to say, 'That would be very nice,' but my voice came out as no more than a whisper.

He shook his head slowly and then smiled.

I took the glass he offered me filled with wine from the bottle he had chilling in the cooler on the sideboard, but was shaking so much I had to steady it with both hands.

For a moment the thought occurred to me that the wine might be poisoned or drugged, but if Gabriel did have any evil intentions towards me then not drinking the wine wouldn't save me. I sipped it slowly though my natural instinct, especially in the circumstances, was to swallow it all in one go.

Gabriel sat down on the other sofa opposite me, toying with his glass, not drinking.

Strange what you notice when you're absolutely terrified. Like how long and elegant his fingers were as they curved round the glass which sparkled in the glow from the lamps. Wondering if the wine glasses were genuine crystal, as if that made any difference to my present situation.

For a few moments we sat there quietly, with me drinking the wine increasingly quickly till to my astonishment I saw the glass was almost empty. Gabriel didn't touch his, but suddenly he broke the silence, causing me to jump and spill the last few drops of wine over my jacket. If he noticed, he gave no indication.

'Well, Alison, I suppose you didn't expect to find me here.'

As a statement of the obvious this was hard to dispute.

Goodness knows how, but I managed to find my voice, though the words still came out in no more than a whisper, 'I thought I'd come to see George.'

Gabriel raised his eyes to the ceiling then leaned back and frowned at me.

'Ah, yes, George – you came to see George. Instead you found me. Gabriel Santos - the man who died all those years ago, who drowned in the pond on Hampstead Heath.'

Somehow I summoned up the courage to reply, 'I'd a feeling you were still alive Gabriel, even though all the evidence was to the contrary. When I saw you on that train last November, I was convinced it was you.'

'Yes,' he replied regretfully, 'I suppose it had to happen at some time, someone from the past had to see me. And we thought Glasgow would be safer than London.'

By now my curiosity was beginning to overcome my fear.

'But why did you agree to meet me? After all I'd no evidence it was you, only what I saw and a gut feeling. You could easily have put me off, given me some story.'

He looked at me as though I'd said something very odd, but remained quiet, toying with the glass.

I hurried on, unable to stand the silence, 'After all these years without contact, I wouldn't have been surprised if George had forgotten me, or not particularly wanted to see me.'

Gabriel shook his head. 'I don't think you're the kind of person who is easily put off, Alison. Even if "George" had refused to see you.' He smiled, took a sip of wine and said, 'You would have found some other way. After all someone who goes to all the trouble you've gone to is a very determined person.'

He paused and then sighed, 'You wouldn't have rested until you'd solved the mystery and I still wanted to be in control, to know what you were up to. If you were willing to go all the way to London, were willing to track down the others in that house in Hampstead....' His voice tailed off. He didn't mention Kara's name.

'How did you know that, what I'd done?'

I was astonished. Had he been following me? Perhaps that sighting at the Theatre Royal wasn't by chance after all.

'I have my sources. How do you think I've managed to lie low all this time?'

I thought about everything that had happened. Why had he said 'we'? Someone had been covering up for Gabriel and it had to be either Melanie or Josie. Yes, that would explain so much.

There was nothing to be lost now by asking him outright.

'Who was it, Gabriel? Was it Josie? Or Melanie? They're the only two people who've been involved in my attempts to find out the truth.'

He shook his head ruefully. 'That's for me to know,' he said. He winked at me, obviously enjoying my discomfort.

'So are you going to tell me what happened, Gabriel?'

If he was going to murder me (I was now sure he'd murdered poor George), I might as well have the satisfaction of knowing the true story.

'Some of it you must have guessed - or guess,' he replied with an unusual flash of humour. 'For one thing - I'm not dead.'

'But George is...' I blurted out the words without pausing to think.

'Of course. But that was ...convenient.'

The old cold, detached Gabriel was back. I wasn't convinced by the use of the word 'convenient'.

He must have seen the look of disbelief on my face. 'Tsk, tsk. Do you think I murdered poor George? Let's just say his death was... helpful.'

Why did I not believe him? Gabriel had been the one to go up to the Heath to look for George. Or was that a cover story too?

'Kara said it was your body. She identified you after you drowned.'

I stumbled over the words as he tapped the side of his wineglass.

'Ah, yes, Kara. What else could she say? She had no choice.'

'That's ridiculous, Gabriel. Of course she had a choice.'

I was now angry with him, my fear forgotten. Here was someone who had in all likelihood murdered a friend and destroyed goodness knows how many other lives.

There was a moment's silence and then he laughed, a mocking, mirthless laugh.

I lifted my handbag as if to leave, not at all sure he would allow me to go.

'I don't know what the truth is Gabriel, but Kara for some reason decided to help you.'

His voice was soft, silky.

'Of course she did, little Alison. She could hardly betray her own husband, could she?'

THIRTY-ONE

My new found courage suddenly deserted me. It was as though my whole body had seized up, and I almost fell back on to the sofa. This must be true, it explained so much. Why Kara hadn't evicted him, for one thing.

It was too complicated for me, too far in the past. I should have left well alone, not become involved. It was enough to know I was well and sane, that I hadn't been imagining seeing Gabriel.

Now I had to find a way to escape, get out of the flat and away from him.

'Honestly, Gabriel, perhaps I should forget all this. I really don't know if it's worth my while finding out what happened all those years ago. I've proved to myself I wasn't imagining it was you I saw. That's all that matters.'

I was powerless, powerless to change the past. My only concern should be the present and I quietly berated myself for pursuing a ghost from those far off days. This was why Josie and Melanie had tried to warn me off, but in my stubborn way I'd paid no attention.

'It's a bit late now, Alison, for that. Sit down, please.'

This was a command, not a request. Even so, in spite of my trembling, my head buzzed with questions. What was Gabriel planning to do? Would Susie remember to phone? Would I ever see Simon or the children again? How would my fifth year class cope with their revision without me? All sorts of ridiculous jumbled thoughts came and went.

To my horror Gabriel stood up and came over and sat beside me and leaned in intimately. But his closeness was only another sign he was trying to frighten me.

'You have to understand, Alison,' he said gazing into my eyes and taking one of my hands in his, 'I had enemies, because of who I was and what I did. I couldn't afford to take chances.'

'And yet you did, Gabriel, both with George and with Melanie.'

This time Gabriel got up and went over to stand at the large bay window to gaze out at the view over the residents' garden, now disappearing in the fading light.   Strange to think that out there, in the dusk of a winter's afternoon, people were going about their normal Sunday business. At this moment I would have given anything to be one of them.

'It was all so convenient. I had to disappear and George happened to have an accident.'

This time he laid a light stress on the word "accident", or was that my imagination?

He turned back to face me again.

'So you see, Alison, George's death was a chance for me to get a new identity, a new life. I couldn't let that pass now, could I?'

Any reply would have been inadequate. Nor could I pluck up the courage to ask what exactly had happened to George for fear of provoking some terrible reaction. For all I knew I was trapped in this flat in Hyndland with a complete madman.

'You were in love with George?'

His eyes narrowed.

'Let's not discuss that, Alison. George got himself involved in the gay scene up at Hampstead Heath. I did try to warn him but…' He gave a shrug.

Was he trying to persuade me he was some kind of good guy, only concerned for George's welfare? That was a tall story, very hard to believe.

'But what, Gabriel?'

His voice was cold, detached, with suppressed anger.

'Blackmail is an ugly game, no matter how hard up you are.'

So that was part of the story. George had found out something about Gabriel, had been blackmailing him.

Forcing my voice under control I replied, 'You've been living as George ever since?'

He nodded, almost casually, as if it were of little consequence.

'Wasn't that difficult, didn't anyone miss George?'

Gabriel smiled.

'Oh yes, but I was lucky. George's only living relative was an elderly aunt in Surrey and she was happy with the occasional postcard and Christmas present until she passed on.'

'Surely it wasn't as easy as that.'

I wasn't at all convinced by his story and its apparent simplicity.

'No, it wasn't easy, I wouldn't say it was easy, Alison, but it was preferable to the alternative which was possibly being locked up for a very long time or deported to a fate I prefer not to think about.'

He smiled at me as he sat down again and stretched back lazily on the sofa. For a split second he reminded me again of Kara's cats.

'And I did have a friend.'

So I had been right about that. Someone had been helping Gabriel all these years, had known what he was up to.

'Yes,' I retorted angrily, 'poor Kara. We all wondered why she didn't just kick you out, Gabriel. At one time we imagined Kara might have felt sorry for you, but we had it all wrong.'

Somehow, in my anger, what I meant to say and the questions I wanted to ask weren't coming out as intended and he'd offered no further explanation of the comment about being Kara's husband.

'Well, you were partly right, I suppose.' He shook his head. 'It was a great pity she also died.'

I toyed with my drink, and then downed the dregs in one gulp, warm as it now was.

'Would you like another drink?'

Again I had this bizarre sensation of being two old friends having a pleasant reunion. 'No thanks.' Time to seize my chance to leave. 'I'd better be going; Simon will wonder where I am. We're going out to-night with friends, very punctual friends.'

I rambled on, trying to make him understand I was expected at home and that, unlike poor George, someone would miss me if I didn't return. Though since we weren't actually going anywhere that night I'd no idea how long it would really be before Simon noticed my absence. It was all down to Susie to remember her promise to phone.

I had to try to come up with some scheme to get out of here. Now I knew he was real, I'd no expectation Gabriel would let me walk out.

As though in answer to my unspoken question, Gabriel said, 'Ah, yes, Alison.' But he made no move.

Panic stricken, unable to think clearly, my only thought was to escape, but I couldn't think how. Gabriel might be waiting to the opportunity to spring on me and I'd be totally defenceless.

Even now, in spite of my terror, my natural inquisitiveness wouldn't let me rest, having come this far. 'Gabriel, why did you want to see me? Aren't you going to ask me what I intend to do with this information?'

He smiled that enigmatic smile of his and looked down at me.

'It doesn't really matter, Alison, because I've decided it's time for me to move on.'

To my great surprise he leaned over, took my hand in his and kissed it lightly.

This was becoming harder and harder, but we couldn't sit here like this all afternoon. Then I had a brainwave.

'Gabriel, I'll have to go to the toilet. Where is it?' Surely he wouldn't follow me there?

'Second door on the left at the bottom of the hall,' he said.

I stood up with all the control I could muster, trying not to let my fear show. I'd only have one chance at this and left my handbag on the sofa to give the impression I intended to return.

Gabriel's flat was identical in layout to so many others of this era and the important thing was that the toilet was almost beside the front door.

I walked deliberately slowly down the hallway, trying to appear calmer than I felt, opened the toilet door and waited a couple of moments before operating the flush and running the sink taps at full strength. That would give me a couple of minutes to open the front door and make my escape. Leaving my handbag behind would be a small price to pay.

Trying hard to avoid making the smallest sound I came out of the toilet, tiptoed to the front door and little by little turned the handle. It wouldn't budge.

Another attempt, now pulling and pushing as hard as I could, no longer caring about making a noise, but still there was no movement. Gabriel must have locked it behind me when I came in.

I stopped and listened, but all I could hear was the loud thudding of my heart. A quick look round the hallway yielded nothing that would help me break the lock. I turned back, tried rocking it back and forth, but with no result. The lock didn't budge even a fraction of an inch.

By now I was almost at screaming pitch, ready to weep with terror and frustration when suddenly Gabriel's hand came round and covered mine.

'I wouldn't try that if I were you, Alison.'

THIRTY-TWO

'It's much easier if you unsnib it.'

With a deft movement, Gabriel pulled back the latch. He was smiling, making fun of my discomfort and stupidity.

He handed me my bag.

'Goodbye, Alison. I don't suppose you'll ever really understand the whole story. But be sure of this - we'll never meet again.'

Before I knew what was happening, I was out of the flat, down three flights of stairs and into the street, blinking in the remaining light, feeling as weak as if I'd gone several rounds in a boxing ring, lucky to have escaped. I leaned against the wall for support, breathing deeply, trying to regain my strength.

One question had been answered but there were still so many remaining. Gabriel was still alive, but what had really happened to George? Should I go to the police? And say what?

There was no more to be done here, so, trying to make sense of my muddled thoughts, I went back to my car, narrowly avoiding bumping into a cyclist on my way across the main road.

Half way home I suddenly remembered I hadn't gone anywhere near the dress boutique that had been my original excuse and now would have to think of yet another lie for Simon.

All I'd learned that afternoon swirled round in my head, but none of it made sense. If Gabriel had been Kara's husband, surely it was no more than a marriage of convenience. And why all the secrecy? Josie and Melanie knew more than they were telling me, that was for sure.

When I cast my mind back to my conversations with them it dawned on me they had been more interested in what I knew and any snippets they'd given me were no more than a way of teasing this out. There was something important about all of this, but at the moment I'd no idea what. The answer was there, tantalisingly out of reach, locked somewhere in my memory.

What about George: how had he really died? There was no way Gabriel could have stepped so easily into his shoes, not without help, despite the story he'd tried to spin me.

I reached home no further forward and had only just opened the front door when the phone rang. It was Susie. 'Don't you remember, Alison, you asked me to call you,' she said.

'Yes, of course,' I replied, striking my forehead.

She was agog to find out what had happened.

'I'm fine, that's all that matters,' but she was not to be put off so easily.

'Come on, Alison, what's going on? First you ask me all that stuff about finding out if this Gabriel is really dead, and then you freeze me out while you go round looking like a zombie. You phone me up out of the blue to ask me to cover for you and to take action in case anything should happen to you. Yet you expect me meekly to back off as the story gets interesting? No way. You should know me better than that.'

'Yes, Susie, you're right,' I sighed, with no option but to tell her what had happened. But not now, not right at this moment. All I wanted to do was lie down in a darkened room and recover from my meeting with Gabriel.

'Tell you what,' I said. 'How about we go out for a cup of tea straight after school tomorrow? I promise to tell you everything then.'

'Fine,' she replied grudgingly, 'if you don't try and put me off again. You know I can be as persistent as you.'

I laughed. 'That at least we have in common, Susie.'

'All the clothes in the boutiques were far too young for me,' I said when Simon asked what I'd bought. Possibly he was relieved I hadn't been indulging the credit card, since we hadn't quite managed to pay off the expenses of Christmas.

Gabriel consumed my waking thoughts. I was slightly wiser than six months ago, knowing Gabriel was still alive, but this information didn't help me remember what had been happening in Kara's house. One question answered only led to others: why Gabriel had released me so easily and why he had agreed to meet me at all.

For the rest of the evening this terribly empty feeling lingered, almost as if I'd been bereaved, trying to make sense of what had happened to George. Had there been an accident, or worse, a murder? Was it true he was blackmailing Gabriel and that was why he died? What could be important enough to warrant blackmailing Gabriel?

Susie couldn't help, couldn't dispel my gloom. When we met up towards the end of the school day on Monday she was unusually curt.

'For goodness sake, Alison, cheer up. You're looking terribly down. Surely the third years can't be all that bad.'

She immediately regretted her action, I'm sure, because she touched my arm sympathetically saying, 'Sorry, Alison, I'm the one who's had the bad day. Come on, let's go and have a restoring cup of tea.'

We headed over to Gina's as soon as school was over.

When I finished telling her as little as was reasonable to satisfy her curiosity, she leaned over the table, almost knocking over the remains of my tea.

'Do you know what I think, Alison? None of this, whatever it may be, has anything to do with you. The problem may be that there is no problem. Whatever they were up to, you didn't enter into their thinking at all. That's why it's so difficult for you. I daresay there was something happening; there might even have been a murder. But what can you do about it now? There's absolutely no way you can prove anything.'

She sat back, wagging her finger at me. 'My advice is this - let it go. Forget it. No matter what's happened, you can't change anything. Your memory functioned perfectly well before you saw this Gabriel. You did make a good recovery from the accident, you can be certain of that. Don't torture yourself trying to remember what doesn't concern you.' This last order so fiercely said I was taken aback.

'Now,' she said briskly, 'do you fancy another cuppa?'

I gazed at her in astonishment and started to speak, to say it wasn't all quite as easy as she imagined to let it go, but she shook her head warningly, 'Leave it, Alison.'

We finished our tea, chattering nineteen to the dozen, inspired by a kind of false gaiety.

Later, as I sat in the staffroom, doing my best to concentrate on the pile of fourth year essays, what Gabriel had said about Kara came back to me. "It was a pity she also had to die." I thought I was going to faint, had to put my head down on the desk for a few moments to stop the light-headedness.

Had Gabriel let slip that Kara's death hadn't been as we believed, the result of her heavy smoking, but deliberate in some way? If so, he must have had something to do with it. For some reason she posed a threat to him. There was no way I could stop now - not until I'd found out the truth.

THIRTY-THREE

'What's wrong with you?' said Simon. 'You seem to be living in another world these days. I thought you were over that Gabriel business?'

'I'm fine. I'm thinking about a problem at school. I've a lot on my mind, that's all.' More lies.

'Oh, well, if you want to keep it to yourself that's fine, but whatever's troubling you, it's making you very difficult to live with.'

He rustled his paper deliberately to let me know what he thought of my lame excuse.

Too scared to confront him, having no idea how to tell him of my suspicions, it would be better to say nothing. Besides, there was no real evidence. Every time I tried to sort out the muddle, I ended up with a headache.

One morning in early April I woke up feeling wretched after yet another sleepless night and lay for a few minutes before coming to a decision. I'd see Josie or Melanie again and demand a few answers about Gabriel. I was certain they knew the truth.

Josie was the person to start with, though I had to phone her at the office as that was the only number she'd given me.

She was off on a business trip and wouldn't be back till Thursday, explained her secretary, which left me with no option but to spend a few fretful days trying to put it all out of my mind, to focus on other things, and not succeeding.

Early on the Friday morning I phoned her number again before leaving for school, and to my great surprise she seemed genuinely pleased to hear from me.

'Alison, how are you?'

My intention had been to tell her what had happened, but somehow going into the details of the meeting with Gabriel over the phone wasn't the right way to enlist her help. After a few pleasantries, I came out with my carefully rehearsed statement.

'Josie, I've been thinking about getting in touch with Melanie again. Do you have a contact number? The one she gave me keeps ringing out.'

There was a fractional pause and then Josie said in a more frosty tone, 'I don't think that will be possible, Alison.'

This response could only be because she had suddenly realised that I was still looking for answers, that I hadn't given up.

Even so, this wasn't what I'd expected, given that it was Josie who'd put me in touch with Melanie in the first place.

The only option was to absolutely honest.

'Look, Josie I've no idea what this is all about, what's going on. I'm totally confused about the past - and even more so about the present.'

I hesitated. What the heck. There was only one way to make progress, to force her into helping me. 'I've met Gabriel.' There it was, out in the open.

The intake of breath at the other end of the phone was audible. A long pause before she replied, 'I see.'

Another silence, then, in a slightly more conciliatory tone, 'Don't you have an Easter break soon? Why don't you come down to London? I think you'll find all the answers you want this time.'

'Fine. I'm sure Maura will be delighted to put me up.' How would I manage to wait until Easter? It would appear there was no choice.

'Josie, won't you tell me what's going on?' I pleaded.

But she was not to be drawn, not to be moved. There was a note of bitterness in her reply, 'You deliberately became involved in this, Alison, though both Melanie and I tried to put you off. Tried to let you down gently. It's all gone too far now. I think you have to come to London. You'll understand everything then.'

Finally we agreed I'd phone Josie as soon as I arrived and we'd arrange to meet up. Hopefully she'd keep her promise, because I'd this quite irrational feeling the end of my quest was in sight, that after all this time my questions would find an answer.

Simon's reaction to my news was one of astonishment. 'You're doing what?' He looked upset. 'You're going to London again? Look, Alison, is there something you're keeping from me? It's not this stupid Gabriel business is it? I thought that was all sorted. You know you're absolutely fine - why go upsetting yourself, bringing back bad memories.' A hint of a threat. 'If you go on like this you will end up with problems again.'

It was on the tip of my tongue to tell him everything when he suddenly continued in a different tone of voice, 'Is there something wrong with Maura?'

'No, she's fine. I just want to go to London, to check a few things out, that's all.'

'I'd hoped we'd be able to go away together for a few days. Down to Bute, to enjoy some sea air. Get all this stuff from the past out of your head, make a new start.'

'We can still go,' I said firmly. 'I've two full weeks of holiday and I don't intend to be in London for more than a couple of days.'

Simon sighed, but I wasn't to be swayed. Even so, the strength of his attempts to dissuade me was worrying. On more than one occasion before I left he said, 'Well, Alison, go if you want to, but on your own head be it.'

The next thing to do was to phone Maura, trying hard to think of a reasonable excuse for a second trip so soon after the first. In the end I thought it best to stick to the truth, or at least a version of the truth.

'I'm going to meet Josie again,' I said. 'I'm curious about some of the things that happened all that time ago when I lived in Kara's house in London and she might be able to help.'

Although I didn't say it, I felt Maura was in part responsible for all that had happened. If she hadn't sent me that article from the *Hampstead and Highgate Express* I would have convinced myself I'd imagined seeing Gabriel, that it had all been a case of mistaken identity.

'There's only one slight problem, Mum. You're welcome to come and use the flat, but Alan and I were planning to go to away for a short break over Easter.'

'Maura, you go ahead with your plans. As long as you don't mind me staying at your flat for a couple of nights then I'll be fine.'

What a stroke of luck that Maura and Alan would be away. There'd be less explaining to do.

Maura sounded dubious. 'Are you sure, I don't like ...'

'There's nothing to worry about.' We spent a few more minutes in general chit-chat before I could persuade her that, yes, I was able to cope and she rang off with final instructions about the fridge and working the microwave.

The Easter break is a busy time of year and the train was crowded so although I'd managed to book a seat at the window, I was squashed in by a family of enormous proportions. It was easy to see how they'd become so large, given that they munched non-stop all the way to Euston.

As best I could I curled into the corner of my seat and buried my nose in my book, though I was too distracted to concentrate. After reading the same page at least three times, I put the book down and, though there was very little to see in the gathering dusk, gazed out of the window, lost in thought, until the train finally drew into Euston station.

Maura had left instructions for every eventuality. 'Mum - set the fridge to 5 if the weather is hot' and 'press the shower button twice quickly as it's a bit quirky' as well as a list of names to be contacted in every possible emergency.

It was early evening, so there was still time to try Josie at her office, but her response wasn't at all as expected. My plan had been to meet her one evening, to question her about what had happened, tell her about my meeting with Gabriel.

'Look, Alison,' she said in a voice that brooked no argument, 'I've taken the day off tomorrow. I think it would be best if you and I paid a visit to Melanie together. That way you'll understand everything. I'll pick you up at Maura's flat at nine thirty. I know where it is.'

The line suddenly went dead, leaving me staring in puzzlement at the receiver, wondering if I was really going to learn the truth at last.

Josie rang early as she'd promised. 'Are you almost ready, Alison?' Her voice was crisp and clear over the line. No niceties, straight to the point.

'Yes, I'm fine Josie and how about you?' I replied, to let her see I didn't consider this very acceptable behaviour, businesslike as it might be.

She ignored this comment, merely said, 'I'm on my way.'

It had been a night of little sleep, hearing in my half asleep state that tune Gabriel had hummed so often and which had so disturbed Kara every time she heard it. What could any of them have had to do with the Paris riots of '68? None of it made any sense.

When Josie arrived promptly to collect me I was desperate to find out where we were going, but she replied to my questions with a curt, 'You'll understand a great deal soon enough Alison; in fact you'll understand it all.'

There was no point in pressing her further. If she was in this kind of a mood, silence was the only option.

Even at this time of the morning, London was busier with traffic than Glasgow in the worst of the rush hour and once again the noise and the bustle of people struck me forcibly as I gazed out of the window.

Much of what we passed through was familiar, but we weren't heading in the direction I'd expected, back into town, to meet up with Melanie at her office. Why were we heading north out of London?

THIRTY-FOUR

Several times I was about to ask where we were going, but one stealthy sideways glance at Josie's face and my courage failed me.

As we travelled further and further away from the city centre she suddenly broke the silence.

'In case you're concerned, Alison, we're heading north, but only as far as Pinner.'

'Why? I didn't think Melanie lived there?'

There was no reply, no explanation as to why Melanie might have moved out to the suburbs of Pinner.

When Josie did speak again, her expression was grim. 'Well, your determination has paid off. When you hear what Melanie has to say, you'll be sorry you didn't drop this business sooner.'

There was no mistaking the anger in her voice, but whether it was directed against me or no more than a vague, general anger I'd no idea.

Even so, I wasn't going to accept this rebuke meekly. Little did she know how much anxiety I'd had over the past few months: unable to sleep, unable to function normally, knowing there was something I should remember, but not being capable of doing so. Feeling my sanity was under threat.

'I think that's unfair, Josie, now I've met Gabriel. No matter who it was Kara identified as the person drowned in the pond in Hampstead, it wasn't him.'

She didn't answer and I went on, 'Surely you understand that when I first saw Gabriel on that train from Edinburgh there was no way I could ignore it. Not when he'd supposedly died

202

so long ago.' Damn Josie. All I'd tried to do was find out the truth, break through the tangled web of deceit in that house in Hampstead, a web that enmeshed us all even yet.

The car wound its way north, up through the clutter of Wembley, past the once modern Northwick Park hospital, now much the worse for wear, through the old town of Harrow on the Hill before we reached the High Street at Pinner.

Suddenly we turned left down a street I didn't recognise and drew up abruptly at a pair of large wrought iron gates. Without looking at me, Josie got out of the car and spoke into the intercom.

The well-oiled gates swung open without a sound and we drove slowly up a winding road shaded by a mixture of large oak and London lime trees, the gloomy, overgrown canopy they made above us making me shiver.

A large redbrick building sat at the end of the driveway. It had the appearance of having once been a fine country house, but not now: the small bronze plaque by the weathered oak door read *St Aethlred's Nursing Home*.

It was only when Josie said, 'We're here, Alison. This is the end of our journey,' I understood with mounting concern my guess that Melanie was very ill had been correct.

Josie pushed the bell on the right-hand side of the door and as we stood there, waiting for a response, I wished I hadn't become involved, had done what everyone had tried to tell me and ignored that sighting of Gabriel in Edinburgh.

What did it all matter now? Whatever had been going on in that house in Hampstead hadn't been any concern of mine then and wasn't now. I knew as much as I needed to: my memory wasn't playing me false, I wasn't ill. There was nothing I could do about the past.

What a fool I was. No wonder Josie had been so cross with me, had tried to make me stop. In my usual headstrong way I'd refused to listen, had been so certain it was all to do with me.

A stout middle-aged woman wearing a severely cut navy blue suit opened the door, her brief nod indicating she was expecting us.

Inside the building it was cool and tranquil. A long wood panelled corridor, discreetly lit by soft lamps, led to a comfortable waiting area furnished in English Country house style with big squashy sofas and thick curtains complete with swags and tails, all in restful shades of green and blue. But this was no smart hotel. The smell of death was in the air, that slightly sickly smell of decay that no amount of pot pourri or air freshener can disguise.

I shuddered, wondering why Josie had brought me here. She went over and spoke quietly to the receptionist at the desk beside the waiting area.

'We've come to see Melanie.'

The receptionist smiled at Josie, a smile of recognition. She asked us to sign in and directed us to the seating area before speaking quietly into the internal telephone.

A few minutes later a young woman in a crisp navy and white uniform came bustling down the corridor, tucking in the stray blonde curls escaping from her starched cap.

'So you're visiting Melanie. I'm so glad. She doesn't have many visitors apart from your friend. She'll be really pleased to see a new face.'

The uniformed nurse kept up a steady stream of chatter as we followed her down the corridor, all the way up in the noiseless lift until we reached Melanie's room on the third floor. This was it, I thought. This was my last chance to have some answers - if I could manage to find the right questions.

The nurse paused for a moment, listened and then knocked, putting her head round the door without waiting for a reply.

'Visitors for you, dear. You weren't sleeping or anything, were you?'

She turned to us.

'Now if you want anything, call me. Don't tire her too much. The buzzer is by Melanie's bed.'

With that she bustled off, leaving us alone with the frail figure on the bed.

'Come over and sit down.'

The voice seemed to come from deep within the bedclothes. She showed no surprise at seeing me, so my guess about Josie was correct. Finding her like this grieved me greatly. Melanie was more than sick: here I was in the presence of death.

Josie bent over and kissed the thin, almost transparent, cheek.

'I've brought Alison to see you.'

It seemed impossible to believe that a few weeks could make so much difference. Melanie had been thin when I saw her last, but now it was as though she was no more than a shadow cast on the white sheets.

A bony hand grasped the cover as though for support. 'It's all right. Come nearer Alison, I won't bite you.' A touch of the old humour.

I leaned over and kissed her lightly, feeling her skin dry and papery beneath my touch, but could think of nothing appropriate to say and in my cowardly way left Josie to do the talking.

We sat one on either side of the bed, leaning forward to catch her words.

'What brings you here, Alison?' she asked in a faint husky voice as she struggled to sit up.

Fortunately Josie spoke first.

'Alison wants to know the truth about Gabriel, find out what really happened all those years ago.'

A trace of a smile flickered across Melanie's face. 'The truth? Does any one of us really know the truth?' She started to cough, that terrible racking cough I'd first heard when we met in the Glasgow restaurant and which had so alarmed me then.

Josie eased her into a sitting position and within a few minutes the coughing fit had passed, but it had taken its toll as she lay back in the bed, exhausted.

'Why didn't you tell her Josie? There was no need to bring her all this way to see me. You know all about it.'

'Because only you really know the whole truth, Melanie. And besides, she's seen Gabriel - and seen you with Gabriel.'

Josie was speaking to Melanie but she was looking over in my direction.

'It's time to let go of the past.'

THIRTY-FIVE

For a moment Melanie's dull, clouded eyes flared into life. 'Gabriel? Is that not ended yet?'

'No, Melanie, it's not. That's why you must tell Alison everything, so that she will understand and take what action she considers necessary.'

'I'd like some water.'

Josie tenderly raised Melanie's head so that she could drink more comfortably from the glass, but after a few sips she fell back again, as though the effort had exhausted her.

'What do you want to know Alison? What can I tell you?'

Now the opportunity to learn the truth had finally arrived, I was at a loss.

'Well, anything you remember,' I said lamely.

Josie looked at me and said, 'We can't tire her out. Her reserves are very low.'

But it was too late for caution. I needed some answers, some honest answers and said in a rush, 'What was it about Gabriel? Why did Kara allow him to stay on the house - or come there in the first place? Did he have some kind of hold over her?' Gabriel had told me he was Kara's husband, but was it another of his lies?

More questions tumbled out. 'What about George? What was the connection? Was George's death really an accident?' It was as though a dam had burst and all my pent up frustration spilled out.

'Steady, Alison, take it slowly,' said Josie in some alarm, looking again at Melanie.

Melanie raised her hand. 'It's all right, Josie,' she whispered. 'I understand Alison's desperation to find out. After all she's been trying hard all these months.'

She lay back on her pillow, her breathing shallow and quick, as though garnering her remaining strength.

'Kara took Gabriel in because she had no choice. He was her husband, wanted by the French police in connection with the Paris riots of 1968. And he was under suspicion of murder. That's why he came back to Hampstead when she thought he'd gone for good, why he laid low. Goodness knows how he managed to get out of Paris without being caught.'

This was difficult to believe, then I remembered my glimpse of Gabriel on the video at school, confirming her story about the Paris riots. 'But why did Kara not kick him out or inform the police? It wasn't a real marriage,' I replied, thinking about the living arrangements in the house.

Melanie took a moment or two to reply, looked over at Josie and then shook her head.

'Kara was in trouble herself. Her real name was Katerina Zelenka. She was from Czechoslovakia but she came to this country illegally. Gabriel knew that. He had a lot to lose, but so had Kara.' Ah, that explained Kara's reluctance to be photographed.

Each answer raised another question.

'How did they come to be married? I mean Kara was a lot older than he was.'

It was Josie who replied, with an anxious glance at Melanie.

'They met through their mutual friends in the international Marxist movement. They were both dissidents after a fashion. That was the connection. It was a marriage of convenience for both, but by the time Kara found out what he'd really been up to it was too late, she was too involved herself.'

'And George,' I turned back to Josie, 'I thought that Melanie said Gabriel was... interested in George?'

'Oh, he was,' Josie replied quickly before Melanie could answer. She was trying to help, to fill in the bits of the story she knew well, 'but Gabriel was interested in a few people. Even you must have known where George's preferences lay.'

Since I'd never given George's love life a thought this was news to me, but I nodded in agreement anyway. It was difficult to believe I hadn't recognised why his social life centred so much on the Hampstead scene. Even in those supposedly liberated days George would have been at pains to keep his private life exactly that - private.

She went on, 'That's what caused the problem with Kara. Gabriel reappeared in her life when she thought she'd got rid of him for good after her spell in hospital. She was sure she was safe, but he turned up and started an affair with George under her nose.'

'You both knew all this was going on? Why didn't I suspect?'

Josie shrugged. 'I didn't understand everything that was happening then either. And Melanie,' a quick glance at the silent figure on the bed, 'had no reason to suspect.'

Was she telling the truth even now? I recalled that episode long ago in Kara's kitchen when I'd seen Josie and Simon sitting at the kitchen table, heads bent close together, talking intimately.

Melanie seemed exhausted again and was lying back with her eyes closed, but she whispered, 'Josie was the one who understood most. I wonder how I could have missed so much.'

That makes two of us, I thought, waiting for one of them to speak again, but when the silence continued said, 'Poor George. He must really have had a bad time of it.' Anger on behalf of George welled up, choked me.

'Good grief, no, Alison. You must have realised what was going on: all that time George spent up in those Hampstead pubs and probably the Heath itself. That's how he came to be there the night he drowned.'

If it hadn't been for the circumstances I'd have suspected this was all wildly exaggerated, but Melanie had nothing to lose by lying to me now.

It helped make sense of so many of the bits of the puzzle.

'So was George's death an accident? Or murder?'

Josie shrugged, then said, 'Who knows? You remember that at heart Kara was kind. She worried about George; she thought he was young and vulnerable. She was concerned about some of the company he kept, even before the Gabriel affair. When he didn't return that night she insisted Gabriel go look for him because she realised Gabriel would know where to find him.'

'It couldn't have been as simple as that.'

This was all too plausible, too glib, almost as though it had been rehearsed.

Josie ignored this comment and continued, 'Gabriel said when he eventually ended up at the Heath there were police everywhere. A man walking his dog had seen the body floating in the water. Of course Gabriel recognised immediately it was George and saw an opportunity to solve all his problems at a stroke. Or that was the story.'

Her tone of voice made it clear she also found it hard to believe this version of events. After a pause she added, 'There was some notion that George had found out Gabriel's secret and was blackmailing him.'

'So it was murder, then?'

Josie shook her head. 'Who knows? Or cares?'

'I cared...and still care,' I muttered. 'I thought I was losing my mind.'

Melanie opened her eyes. She'd obviously been listening to all that was said and I had to lean forward to catch her words.

'Don't judge Kara too harshly for this, Alison. After all, when Gabriel came straight back and told her what had happened and what he wanted her to do - to identify the body as his - she finally saw a way of getting rid of Gabriel for good. What did it matter to poor George? He was dead anyway.'

There were still too many loose ends, too many puzzles.

'There was still the question of justice, Melanie.'

Neither of them responded to this.

How much could I believe? If Melanie knew the truth about Gabriel when they were living in that house, why had she become involved with him at all? And if she didn't, how had Josie found out? How could Gabriel so easily take over George's identity?

As if in answer to my unspoken questions Melanie suddenly resumed her story.

'I met Gabriel again a number of years ago when I was back over from New York. Much in the way you did, Alison.'

A shadow crossed her face as though the recollection pained her.

'Quite by chance I was in Edinburgh for a conference and Gabriel turned up at the same conference - as George King of course.'

She looked at me sadly, 'We met, we became lovers, and then a few years ago I became ill.'

It was only a guess, but if I was right, her illness was all because of Gabriel. No wonder Josie was so bitter, but it didn't explain why she was still involved after all this time.

In the silence that followed I wondered if asking more questions would make me seem heartless. As if guessing what was in my mind, Melanie whispered, 'Alison, there are other things you want to know. I'll try to help you if I can, but I don't have all the answers.'

I felt the tears pricking my eyes and brushed them away impatiently. That would do no one any good, but I had to ask the question, even if it did cause Melanie pain.

'If you knew what Gabriel was like, why did you get involved with him, Melanie?'

She laughed softly. 'That was the problem; I didn't make the connection either, didn't know what he was really like. You must remember how persuasive he could be, how...'she searched for the right word...'how intriguing. Isn't it ridiculous that Josie, whom we all thought of as not at all worldly wise, was the only one really to know what was happening.'

Josie nodded silently in agreement. 'I didn't think to say anything,' she muttered. 'It didn't occur to me that Melanie might become involved with Gabriel. When I found out, it was too late. George had tried to make money once he discovered what Gabriel was up to and look what happened to him.'

Melanie's voice had become a whisper. 'You say you saw Gabriel recently? How is he?'

Josie said to me, 'Gabriel doesn't know about Melanie. She stopped seeing him when the diagnosis was finally made but it was too late for her. There was no doubt that it was Gabriel. The irony is that he should appear to suffer no ill effects, but it's killing Melanie.'

She hesitated. 'You know that Gabriel was into drugs, dealing drugs - that's why George tried to blackmail him.'

'And Melanie...?'

Josie nodded. 'By the time Melanie had decided to break with him, it was too late. When he found out how ill she was, he abandoned her.'

This didn't ring true either, because I was now absolutely certain it was Melanie who'd been with Gabriel that night in the Theatre Royal.

So she wasn't telling Josie the whole truth. And Josie hadn't been the naïve student she claimed, even in those days. Was there no end to this tissue of lies?

Melanie had closed her eyes again and her breathing became shallower.

'Should we ring for the nurse?' I asked Josie in a whisper.

'No, but I think we should go and leave her to sleep. You've got what you came for.'

There was nothing to be gained from arguing, in spite of the fact we hadn't even mentioned what might really have happened to Kara, how she had died, and we tiptoed out, leaving that small thin figure alone. Josie spoke to the nurse as we left and I looked back as she hurried towards Melanie's room.

We left St. Aethlred's and crossed to the car park in total silence, my mind in turmoil. How could all this have happened, without my realising? I'd thought it was all to do with Gabriel and those riots in Paris, not that he was a drug dealer. There were still too many unanswered questions.

We got into the car in silence and started back down that long gloomy driveway.

'Pleased with what you've learned, Alison?' asked Josie as we turned out of the gates and began the journey back into London.

'Not really.' I was angry now. 'Do you believe that Gabriel didn't have anything to do with George's death? It all sounds a bit too convenient to me.'

Josie pulled into the side of the road and stopped the car, then turned to face me and sighed, 'If you want an honest opinion, no, I don't think George's death was an accident.

213

Gabriel did go out to look for him, but perhaps there was a scuffle or whatever and George ended up in the pond on the Heath. The way it happened was far too convenient for Gabriel, given all the circumstances.'

She paused, looking at me for a response, but I didn't reply, let the silence hang between us until she continued, 'It's my suspicion he was coming on a bit heavy and blackmailing Gabriel about the drug dealing. Anyway, I believe he had a hand in George's death. I was appalled to learn Melanie and he were lovers.'

'That's all there is to it? A straightforward case of blackmail and drugs?'

'It's the truth, Alison, perhaps not what you wanted to hear, but the truth. Go back to Scotland, forget all this.'

'Yes, but.....' I still had questions.

Josie glanced at me. 'What else?'

'How could Gabriel take over George's identity so easily? And did Kara really die from cancer?'

There was a long pause as though she was considering her reply. Ignoring my comment about Kara she said, 'Well, I don't know that it was easy, but remember George had no close relatives and his company had offices everywhere. No doubt Gabriel could concoct some story: a transfer after a spell of sick leave or something. And all George's documents were available at Kara's house for the taking.'

'Surely he must have had some other help to change his life so dramatically?'

'Yes, Alison, he did have help.'

'So it wasn't you or Melanie ....or even Kara?'

She laughed mirthlessly and then frowned.

'How would any of us have the resources to do something like that? It needs skill and a bit of money in the right places.'

'So what's your guess?' Someone must have helped Gabriel: someone with a good reason.

Josie hesitated again, and then seemed to come to a decision.

'Look, Alison, this isn't really for me to say. Why don't you ask Simon?'

THIRTY-SIX

All the worries about Simon now began to resurface and I thought back to those conversations we'd had about Gabriel: his reluctance to talk about my concerns, his attempts to put me off and the strange phone call from the station phone kiosk.

If Josie was right, Simon was the key to this whole business about Gabriel. Surely this was nonsense; there was no reason on earth why Simon would have anything to do with helping Gabriel evade the law.

His only concern was my health, that I didn't have a relapse after years of being fully recovered from the trauma of the car accident.

Even so, I kept going over and over the same old ground as we drove back to Maura's flat in silence, Josie ignoring any attempts to coax her to give me any further clues. We could speculate as much as we wanted about Gabriel and his motives, but there was no way to prove anything. There would be no point. And nothing we could do would help Melanie.

Josie dropped me at the entrance to Maura's flat. We said a brief farewell and I stood and watched as she drove off, lingering long after her car had disappeared from sight into the crush of traffic on the High Street, knowing this would be the last time I'd see Melanie or Josie.

There were so many people involved in this Gabriel affair, but my first action had to be to pluck up my courage and confront Simon as Josie had suggested. Easy to say, but impossible to decide what to ask him. There was no way to make sense of everything that had happened, of the stories I'd been told - especially how my husband could have had any involvement in this whole sorry episode.

It was my own fault for being so inquisitive, for getting caught up in this madness. Even if Simon wasn't a part of it all, there was no way we could go back to what we were, have the relationship we'd enjoyed before this shadow came between us.

Although I'd agonised all the way back in the train, gone over and over all the possible options, in the end there was no choice but to tell him everything. It might be one way of discovering the answer to this story and what he'd had to do (if anything) with Gabriel taking over George's identity.

The questions I'd rehearsed didn't come out as planned, of course, partly because I hedged round, trying to make out my determination to seek out the truth about the past had been little more than a flight of folly.

'I'd no idea what I'd let myself in for,' I said. 'I thought it was all quite simple. Either I'd seen Gabriel or I'd imagined it. And if I'd imagined it, was it because my memory was playing tricks on me, was I ill again?'

He didn't say much, but let me ramble on, though he did comment that I was "bloody stupid" to have gone off in pursuit of the truth about some "damn fool ghost" without at least letting someone know of my plans.

When it came to the crunch, the opportunity to accuse him, I couldn't do it. This was Simon, my husband who had always had my best interests at heart. There seemed no point in enlightening him about my pact with Susie when I'd gone to meet 'George'. How could I probe him about what Josie had suggested? And Simon would have some other explanation for that mysterious phone call. He would tell me all about it in his own good time.

Worn out by going over and over the possibilities, completely exhausted, I gratefully accepted the gin and tonic he poured for me. There was a time when I'd have preferred a glass of chilled white wine, but I'd gone off that somehow.

Motley came purring around as if he was truly glad to see me and sat on my lap throughout the evening, protesting vigorously every time I made a move to dislodge him.

It was growing late when Simon said, 'Leave it alone, Alison. You've got what you wanted - the truth, or at least as near to the truth as possible. If you don't owe it to yourself you owe it to me and to the rest of the family to file it all away. Put it in that drawer in your mind marked "yesterday". That's where it belongs.'

He was right. There was nothing more to be done, no way back to the past, even if I was minded to pursue matters. There were plenty of more urgent matters to deal with at home.

There was one last task before going to bed - to phone Susie. She'd tried to help me, would be waiting anxiously for my call and though not in the mood for lengthy explanations, I could give her a brief update.

Her voice was full of concern as I reached the end of the story.

'Alison, how could you have been so stupid? Surely you realised what you might be getting yourself involved in?'

'Susie, I really had no idea what was happening. It all started because of my need to know if I really had seen Gabriel on that train from Edinburgh, and an even stronger desire to make sure my memory was fully recovered, that I wasn't ill again.'

'It's all right, Alison,' she cut in hastily. 'You can tell me all about it later when you're feeling better.'

'Fine: I'll call you tomorrow.' Then, about to say, 'Perhaps you could come over,' I hastily changed to, 'Perhaps I could drop in to see you? I have to be in town anyway.' Which was partly true.

'No problem, Alison, any time in the morning will do.'

'I'm off to bed,' I said to Simon, but he merely grunted from behind his book.

The next day, before going round to see Susie and while Simon was out collecting the newspapers, I tried ringing Gabriel at his flat with no clear idea of what to say.

There was no reply and no answering machine either.

By the time I reached Susie's I'd made up my mind. I had to see Gabriel for the last time. I was no longer afraid of him, was merely angry on behalf of Melanie and of all those people who had come into contact with him in that house in Hampstead.

Like a stone cast into a still pond, the ripples he'd made had affected all their lives and yet he seemed to care nothing. If he really had murdered George, and possibly Kara, had seduced Melanie into using drugs, was his careless attitude, his lack of concern, surprising?

Suitably chastened by her last response, this time I did tell Susie of my plans in some detail, but determined not to be swayed by her protests, I made it clear my decision to go round to the flat wasn't up for discussion.

When she realised she couldn't change my mind, she insisted on coming with me.

'I won't come up if you don't want me to, but I will be here in the car.' Her offer of help gave me courage.

There was no answer from Gabriel's flat to my insistent ringing of the buzzer, but I managed to persuade one of the other residents to answer the entry phone and let me in to the main entrance. My steps grew slower and slower as I approached Gabriel's flat. This might turn out to be a very bad idea indeed.

The shrill noise of the bell at Gabriel's main door echoed inside, but no matter how often I pushed it, no one came. The outer storm door was firmly closed and the neighbour in the next flat came out as I started pounding on the door in frustration.

'Can I help you?' he said, no doubt alarmed by the fury of my hammering, wondering what was going on.

I gave him some excuse about having left a book there when I was round some weeks before. It sounded very lame, wasn't much of a reason and he must have wondered exactly how valuable the book was to induce me to attack the door with such vigour.

'I must collect it,' I said with a fierceness unusual for me.

'Well, Mr King has gone, but I could let you in to see if your book is there. I've got the spare set of keys for the landlord,' he said, sounding very reluctant.

As he opened the door, I pushed past him into the flat. It was totally empty. I ran through all the rooms, but they were all deserted.

Not a stick of furniture, not a rug, not a single cup remained and the floorboards echoed to my footfalls. Gabriel had, as he promised, "moved on."

'Did Mr King leave a forwarding address?' I spun round.

The neighbour shook his head, pointing to the pile of letters and junk mail lying behind the door.

'Not judging by the amount of mail that's lying here.'

I could of course have checked at the Post Office, but what was the point of that. What would I do if I found him? It was probably too late even to tell him about Melanie.

It was all over. I knew the truth, or most of it. Anything else would have to remain hidden, in the past.

Suddenly I felt incredibly exhausted as all the adrenaline of the past few months drained away and I stumbled downstairs back to the car where Susie was waiting, tapping her fingers on the steering wheel, fretting about the time I'd been away.

I slid into the passenger seat beside her and put my head back. 'Drop me at home, Susie. I've had enough of all this,' I said.

THIRTY-SEVEN

For us the isle of Bute has the advantage of being within easy reach of Glasgow, yet it's distant enough to have the feel of being on holiday far from the city. Quiet beaches, woodland walks and an abundance of wildlife ensure a holiday to soothe the senses. At the moment that was exactly what we both needed.

'But the weather can be so unpredictable,' said Susie when I told her of my plans. 'Surely you'd be better jetting off somewhere sunnier. There are some good deals at the moment. And although I know the island used to be very popular, surely it's not the best place for a holiday now?'

'No, thank you.' The very thought of the long queues at the airport at this time of year was enough to make me shudder.

'Bute will do nicely. It's still a popular destination and I'm not a sun worshipper like you. If the weather is good, it's a real bonus, but we'll take our waterproofs in case. It's a peaceful few days we're after.'

Susie didn't reply, but her expression made it clear she found it hard to understand my reasoning.

We were in luck. The first day of the holidays the rain, which had been of monsoon proportions for a fortnight beforehand, suddenly stopped, gave way to clear skies with frostier nights. Even so I was glad I'd packed the waterproofs - the Atlantic coast can be very unpredictable and it was better to be prepared.

We'd decided to book into one of the hotels in Rothesay, the main - or indeed the only - town on the island for an extended weekend. That way we'd both have a few days at home before returning to work. Besides, Simon was fretting. The decision about continued funding hadn't had any effect on his stress levels: most likely it all depended on meeting impossible targets. That was the only reason I could think of for his tetchiness, his restlessness.

'Where did I put the charger for my mobile?' he muttered, coming in to the bedroom where I was attempting to cram as much as possible into the one suitcase he had deemed "more than enough" for a few days away.

'Probably still in your study,' I said and he went off to fetch it as I called after him, 'Surely you can afford to be out of touch for a few days? You're supposed to be on holiday.'

If he heard me, he ignored my comment, because there was no response. It was clear to me, as someone who had avoided all attempts to make me buy a mobile phone, that one was fast becoming more than something for dire emergencies.

A smooth crossing on the CalMac ferry from Wemyss Bay to Rothesay restored our good mood. After a quick freshen-up at the hotel we'd chosen on the front with a panoramic view across Rothesay Bay and the boats gently rocking at anchor in the Marina, we headed off for some lunch at the Ettrick Bay tearoom, followed by a walk along the sands towards Kirkmichael. In the gardens of the few houses spaced out along the road, daffodils crowded the flower beds and poked their heads through the grass, nodding vigorously in the breeze.

'I feel better already,' I sighed, lifting my face to catch the warmth of the sun as we wandered slowly along, hoping to work off a very substantial meal.

The beach was almost deserted except for a few parents with young children. On the sands immediately down from the tearoom, one father was exhorting his three children to join him in a race along the shore, but they seemed more interested in digging up the sand and throwing clumps of it at one another.

'I'm glad we're past that stage,' I said, laughing at the dad's attempts to engage the children in a race.

Simon nodded, but he was frowning, still preoccupied. Perhaps he was worried about work, needed more time to feel the benefits of a holiday on the island. I could only hope.

And indeed as the hours drifted past, he seemed visibly to relax as Bute worked its magic and we slowed to the calm pace of life on the island.

We determined to use every minute of sunshine, and in the lengthening evenings stayed out until the gloaming gave way to darkness, strolling back from our evening meal as the sky became peppered with stars.

'I wish we could stay here forever,' I said as we made our way back to the hotel on the last afternoon.

'I doubt it,' Simon smiled. 'You like the city too much to make Bute your permanent home.'

I wasn't so sure. There was plenty do on the island and in winter, when the tourists had gone, we knew the island came alive with activities to suit every interest. And with no traffic jams, no noise, dust or pollution, what did the city have to offer that could compare with this?

Relaxed, at peace with the world, with all thoughts of Gabriel and the mystery of Kara's house well and truly buried, what happened next was a shock, plunging me once more into the darkness of the past.

It came out of something very simple. When we reached the hotel on the last evening, after a long invigorating walk along the shore at St Ninian's Bay, Simon elected to have a shower first. 'I won't take long. Where would you like to eat tonight?' he said.

'Oh, let's go to the Kingarth and we can have a last stroll at Kilchattan Bay afterwards.'

'Done. Let's try to leave about seven? If you can manage to get ready in time,' he said, but he smiled as he spoke.

'You know I'll be much quicker than you,' I protested, acknowledging the joke.

This holiday had been good for both of us, put us back on an even keel, stabilised our relationship which, let's be honest, was beginning to look decidedly shaky.

I lay down on top of the bed and closed my eyes, planning forty winks to restore me for the evening, while Simon was in the shower. About to doze off, I was startled into wakefulness by the sound of a phone ringing and, still half asleep, reached for the hotel phone beside the bed. The ringing continued. For a moment, I couldn't figure out why that might be, then realised the sound was coming from the pocket of Simon's jacket, hanging on the hook on the back of the door.

From the shower room came the sound of hissing water and Simon's slightly out-of-tune singing. I've no idea what made me take the phone from his pocket, except I was still not quite awake. Whatever the reason, I lifted it out and pressed the button to connect to the caller.

'Hello, Simon,' said a voice. 'Have you managed to sort everything out, keep it under control…?' A moment's hesitation. 'Simon? Is that you?'

'It's not Simon…'I managed to say before the line went dead. I pressed the button to ring off and stood there trembling, looking at the mobile as though it would suddenly spring into life again.

Although the conversation (if you could call it that) had been brief, there was something familiar about the voice. Who was it? Someone I'd heard recently.

The shower in the bathroom stopped, and jerked into action, I pushed the mobile back into Simon's pocket and only just managed to fling myself back on to the bed as he emerged from the shower, towelling his hair.

'Your turn, Alison,' he said. It was clear he hadn't heard his phone.

I swung my legs over the edge of the bed and hurried into the bathroom without a word. Should I tell him he'd missed a call? Why was I hesitating?

There was only one reason. With a flash of insight I'd recognised that voice - it was Josie.

THIRTY-EIGHT

Choosing the right moment to ask Simon about the phone call wasn't easy, but as we dined that evening at the Kingarth Hotel, I knew the food would taste like sawdust till I did so.

So, taking a deep breath and hiding behind the pretence of studying the menu I said, 'Oh, by the way, Simon, while you were in the shower, someone rang your mobile.'

I lowered the card in time to see the expression on his face. He was frowning.

'Who was it?'

'No idea. She rang off before I could ask,' I shrugged. The cross look left his face and he sat back. 'Probably work. It would be Marie.' He laughed. 'As well you answered it. I don't want to be involved with any department problems until the holiday is over. Now, have you decided what you want to eat?'

With that he dismissed the call, but I'd the distinct impression this was a deliberate attempt to distract me. He'd evidently forgotten I'd spoken to Marie on the phone several times and her Western Isles accent wasn't easy to mistake.

Then, the more I thought about it, the less certain I became. Perhaps it had been someone else at work, someone who sounded like Josie, a figment of my imagination. Best to forget about it.

It wasn't as simple as that. It never is. When you think everything is settled, fate has a habit of coming in and dealing you a lousy hand.

We returned home to Glasgow the next day and to all appearances I was back to some sort of normality, to the usual daily routine, visiting my mother, keeping the house more or less in order, catching up with the never-ending piles of marking.

Deborah had now decided that living with her parents wasn't a good idea and had moved into the spare room in a flat belonging to one of her friends with a job in banking.

Truth to tell, I wasn't too upset. It would give her a chance to sort out her life without feeling stifled by our expectations of her. And she phoned regularly. All in all I was hopeful that after such a long time everything was settling down.

Life with Simon also fell back into the usual routine and as the days slipped into weeks and all that had happened became a distant memory, I gradually ceased to watch him for signs he might have been involved in the Gabriel story.

There were no more suspect phone calls as far as I could tell, nothing in his manner to suggest I was being monitored. His concern had only been for my welfare: worry I'd become ill again.

I began to feel back to my old self, more relaxed, didn't even want to know who'd helped Gabriel, persuaded myself Josie's remarks about "ask Simon" had been no more than a way of making sure I left London and ceased to trouble her with more questions.

My memory was surely fine, fully restored and that was enough for me: I had to forget the past and think about the future.

The term sped past and the looming summer holidays promised six weeks of freedom, but we'd made no plans about a holiday destination.

'Anywhere except London,' was Simon's firm reply whenever I raised the subject till it became a sort of standing joke between us. It looked very much as if we'd return to Bute. We'd both enjoyed the tranquillity of the island so much at Easter I'd be delighted to spend the summer there. After all I'd been through, the peace and quiet of life away from the city would suit me fine: I'd had enough excitement to last me a lifetime. And, as a bonus, there'd be little chance of bumping into any of my colleagues, or even pupils for that matter: most were booked to much more exotic destinations.

As the last days of term drew near all I could think about was the tranquillity of a walk at Scalpsie Bay to watch the seals on the rocks, a cup of hot chocolate and home-made cake at the Ettrick Bay tearoom, a brisk walk along part of the West Island Way. The sound of a seagull in the city, scavenging for food, and I was on the ferry coming into the calm waters of Rothesay Bay, seeing the curve of houses along the shore, smelling that holiday town mixture of brine, seaweed and fish and chips.

Susie was so beside herself with excitement I was more than a little suspicious about the true purpose of her trip to the Caribbean.

'Don't fuss so much, Alison,' she said innocently after my latest attempt at a discreet enquiry. 'If Ross and I decide to tie the knot, you'll be the first to know.'

This protest didn't convince me. It would be quite in character for Susie to do something mad like get married on a whim on some Caribbean island.

The only remaining difficulty was my mother.

Her own holiday had to be called off when her friend, Jessie McAdam, had to go into hospital at short notice for her long-awaited hip operation.

'That's the National Health Service for you,' she sighed. 'Poor Jessie had been waiting for so long for this operation and now they had to schedule it right at the time we intended to go on holiday.'

I didn't like to point out that this was unlikely to have been done on purpose and that at Jessie's age, I was sure the operation took priority over the holiday.

My mother was still aggrieved about this disruption to her plans and began to drop hints about not knowing when she'd get away, repeating several times how much she'd been looking forward to a change of scene.

She was less enthusiastic when she found out we were destined for Bute and not some more distant location such as Majorca, where she and Jessie had planned to go.

Bute had an added benefit: we could leave Motley at home rather than trying to find a suitable cattery. My next door neighbour, Ella, kindly agreed to look after him and Deborah promised to pop in from time to time.

So arrangements were settled to everyone's satisfaction and I began to feel almost cheerful again, the past and Gabriel no more than a distant memory, locked away.

In early June the weather became hot and sunny. Day after day of sunshine made us all feel happy, except for Harry Sneddon, who in his usual gloomy fashion went round saying, 'It'll never last, you know. This has happened before. Sunny right up to the last day of term, then wham, the first day of the holidays, the rain starts.'

While this may well have been true, his efforts to inject a note of realism totally failed to puncture our high spirits.

The last week of term is the one for clearing up and as the days progress, fewer and fewer children attend until you're left with those who persist in coming in right to the bitter end. They're usually the ones you've hardly seen all year: a kind of perverse logic.

On the Wednesday afternoon, as I was heading along the corridor, laden as usual, I almost literally bumped into Susie. I was on my way to return several videos, fearful of the wrath of the technician if they weren't back in place before the end-of-session stocktaking.

'Steady up, Alison, could you not find one or two willing pupils to share that heavy load?'

'Strangely enough, they all decided they had other things to do at the mention of clearing up. I came back from break to find my last remaining three had disappeared.'

She laughed. 'Let me help you, then. Good heavens, it looks like you've most of the contents of the audiotape library there.'

Indeed I was weighed down by eight or so videos in addition to the usual load of books and papers.

'Yes, I'm trying to return them as stealthily as possible. I'd quite forgotten how many I'd borrowed. If you could help me sneak them back?'

'Let's divide them up then,' suggested Susie, 'and that way it won't look so bad.'

We giggled as we made our way along the corridor.

'I'll see if the coast is clear,' hissed Susie. She put the videos back into my hands and cautiously opened the door of the audio-visual room. 'Great. There's no one there.' She beckoned me in, switched on the light and we started to replace the videos on the shelves.

We were almost finished when the door opened with a thud and Harry Sneddon came bumbling through. 'Oops, sorry, ladies, didn't know there was anyone here,' he apologised.

He looked at us knowingly. 'Sneaking back some videos, eh? Well, I have to confess I'm doing the same myself, especially,' he paused and rubbed his hands together, 'as I've at last been given the word my application for early retirement has been approved.'

'Isn't that a bit sudden Harry? We knew you wanted to retire but surely you need more notice than that?'

Harry winked. 'Yes, but officially I retire on the 20th of August so it's hardly worth returning to school for a few days.'

Another leaving-do to attend, I thought.

Videos duly replaced, Susie and I were on our way out when Harry said in a very matter-of-fact way, 'Oh, Alison, do you remember that video that upset you a few months ago?'

Remember it? How could I forget? I nodded.

'Well,' he said, a wicked gleam in his eye, 'I saw the whole thing through and I think there's something else to interest you.'

No, no, I prayed silently. It's all over, all done with.

As I caught Susie looking at me strangely, I determined not to show any sign of disquiet, and deliberately making my voice sound light, I said, 'Yes, Harry, I think I do remember. What about it?'

He lifted it up in front of me and an involuntary shiver went down my spine at the sight of the cover with the date of 1968.

'Have a look at this bit,' he said. He put the video into the recorder and pressed the play button, winding quickly through the first section before stopping at the scenes of the Paris riots.

There it was again, the shouting mob, Gabriel at the front, so young, so long ago. A part of my past. Why was Harry showing me this? It had nothing to do with me now. 'I've seen this, Harry. It's of no consequence,' I protested. There was no way I was discussing this with Harry. It was none of his business.

'No, wait, Alison,' he said as I turned to leave. 'It's this next part I think you should see.'

Now intrigued in spite of myself, I turned my attention back to the screen. The tape had been wound a bit further on, showing the same crowd viewed from a different angle.

'Look at it carefully,' said Harry, 'and then tell me what you see.'

Quickly I scanned the frame he'd paused, about to say, 'I really have to go, Harry,' when something made me hesitate. I looked, then looked again, unable to believe my eyes.

There, on the fringes of the crowd, at the very back but still unmistakable, was Simon.

THIRTY-NINE

It was impossible to remain in school for the afternoon, pretending nothing had happened, but Susie immediately came to my aid. 'Go home, Alison, I'll speak to the Head and cover for you.'

Too upset to argue, I rushed out, hearing Harry say in a puzzled tone, 'I thought it was Simon. I've only met him a couple of times, but he's not changed much, has he?'

Choking back a reply, I fled, leaving Susie to deal with Harry.

The rush to get home was pointless as Simon wouldn't be back for hours, but that didn't stop me breaking the speed limit and jumping the traffic lights a couple of times.

Josie's words, "Ask Simon" now made sense. To think I'd so carelessly dismissed her comments, had lacked the courage to confront him properly over that call to his mobile while we were on Bute. Now it would appear he was central to the whole story.

The house was silent, empty. Little bits of my life with Simon lay adrift everywhere as I roamed the house, looking for clues, looking for answers. Our wedding photo stood on top of the piano in the sitting room, pictures of us with the children as toddlers and as teenagers were ranged along the walls. I looked at his clothes, scattered over the bedroom, his shaving kit abandoned in the bathroom in his haste to get to work, as though I might find some clue among these personal possessions.

As I picked up a crumpled shirt lying beside the laundry basket and held it against my face, his smell was so familiar to me that for a moment I was overcome and sat down heavily on the bed, the bed we'd shared for so many years. Still clutching the shirt, my tears seeping into the fabric, I tried to think what to do next.

How could this be? Had Simon been involved in some way with this business about Gabriel, had he been deceiving me all these years? I refused to believe it was by chance he'd been in Paris, been in that same rioting crowd, at the same time as Gabriel. Why hadn't he told me when I'd first tried to find out if it really was Gabriel on the train from Edinburgh?

There was something he was hiding from me and with a hollow feeling in the pit of my stomach I wondered if this secretiveness included the true story about his relationship with Josie. There could be no doubt his dismissal of my concerns, my worries over the past months, were more about making sure I didn't find out the truth, rather than some fear about my fragile mental state.

Even as these thoughts came and went between waves of weeping, there was a lingering feeling of guilt, of admitting that in the end I'd told him very little, had missed out important parts of the story. He must have guessed something was afoot. That was why he hadn't made more of a fuss. He'd known only too well what had been going on, because somebody had told him, had warned him.

Then my tears turned to anger. How dare he let me suffer like this? What sort of a marriage had it been with all these secrets between us for so long?

A great sadness suddenly overwhelmed me and for several minutes I was unable to move, before telling myself sternly this would achieve nothing. At this point I needed to be strong, be assertive, if I was ever to find out the truth.

Time ticked past as I sat there, letting my mind roam free over all the events of the past few months, recognising little things that at last began to make sense. The way Simon had claimed he scarcely remembered Gabriel, his dismissal of my first sighting on the Edinburgh train, his determination not to go to London with me, his odd questions. Add to that his call from the phone box at the station, the strange message and the phone call from Josie.

Eventually I stood up and from force of habit began to tidy up, putting clothes in the laundry basket or the cupboard, straightening the duvet cover. I caught sight of my drawn face in the mirror above the chest of drawers, and feeling as if I'd aged about ten years in the last few hours, went in to the bathroom to make a valiant attempt to repair the damage. I tidied my hair and washed my face, applying the brightest lipstick I could find in the bathroom cabinet, but these endeavours only made me look worse than before.

The clock downstairs struck the hour and a few moments later there was the sound of a key in the lock. Thank goodness Deborah had moved out. I didn't need any more complications.

'Hi, Alison, I'm home.'

That so familiar cry would never be the same again. I got to my feet more than a little unsteadily, took a deep breath and made my way slowly downstairs.

He was standing in the hall, shrugging off his outdoor jacket. As he hung it on the peg nearest the door he turned to greet me, but the smile froze on his face as he saw my expression and for a fleeting moment I detected a hint of fear.

'What's wrong?'

His face was dark, rather than concerned.

Was I so easy to read? I'd carefully rehearsed being calm and rational, suggesting a drink before outlining my suspicions to him. I'd gone over and over every possible scenario while waiting for him to return. My first words would be, 'I'm very disappointed, Simon, that you could deceive me like that over this business of Gabriel.'

Then when he made to reply, I'd hold up my hand in a warning fashion. 'No, let me finish, you can have your say later.'

Of course it didn't happen like that. Overwrought with emotion, anger and fear, I opened my mouth to speak and then burst into tears.

My plans were all for nothing because Simon took me in his arms and led me into the sitting room, saying, 'Hush, Alison, it's all right, honestly, it's all right.'

'What do you mean?' I hiccupped, 'It can never be all right between us again.'

To my fury he started to chuckle.

'It's not like you imagine.'

Incensed by his response, I pulled myself away.

'How dare you,' I cried, 'and after all you've put me through.'

He shook his head.

'No, after all you've put yourself through. We all tried to warn you, but you wouldn't listen.'

'But I couldn't remember,' I wailed, sobbing again. 'That was the problem. I knew there was something, but I couldn't remember what. I had to find out if the past was causing me to lose my mind.'

'And,' replied Simon moving towards me again, 'did you find out? Did you remember? Perhaps there was nothing to remember, Alison, at least not in the way you imagined.'

As he went to put his arm round my shoulder, I shrank back. He wasn't going to dismiss my months of frustration as easily as that. I felt betrayed: he would have to have a very good explanation for what he'd done if he wanted to restore my trust.

He sat me down firmly on the sofa and settled himself in the chair opposite, all the time keeping hold of my hands, then lifted my face so that I was looking directly at him.

'Will you pay attention to me, Alison? Listen carefully for a change, instead of rushing off as usual down a blind alley.'

This was more an order than a request and I nodded dumbly, too weak to speak. Was there any way to make everything right again, take us back to how we'd been before this spectre from the past appeared?

He sat in silence for a few moments, as though trying to decide where to start. Eventually he sighed and said, 'Alison, in the 1960s I was one of those students at the L.S.E recruited to look out for any subversives. No, don't shake your head. You can at least remember that. There may not have been the McCarthy witch trials they had in America, but the powers that be wanted to make sure that any radicals likely to cause trouble were kept in check or watched. You must recall what was happening across Europe? The French Government was almost brought down by violent protests and the actions of the workers and the students. Fear of what might happen was everywhere, including Britain. Remember where we met?'

He paused and waited for my answer.

'At a party Josie's friend Sylvia had in that flat on Haverstock Hill,' I sniffled. 'But that was the 70s, not the 60s.'

He ignored my last comment and squeezed my hands again.

'My contacts were through Josie at the L.S.E. Gabriel was the prime suspect I was attached to.'

I wasn't entirely convinced by this story.

'How come I saw you on that video Harry showed me? You were in Paris at the same time as Gabriel, part of those student riots.'

'Yes, I followed him there, kept tabs on him all through the summer of '68.'

A sudden, horrible thought struck me, one I couldn't bear to contemplate.

'Were you just making use of me to keep up surveillance on Gabriel? Did you become involved with me because he was living in the same house? Was that your only reason?'

Then another thought, remembering the incident in Kara's kitchen when I'd seen him with Josie.

'Was it really Josie you were interested in?'

He laughed loudly, then stopped as he saw the look on my face.

'Good heavens, no. Josie was my contact and has been ever since.'

He hesitated again, a bit shamefaced, gazing at me warily, trying to judge my reaction before he resumed the story.

'Well, I have to be honest. In the beginning when we met at that party, I couldn't believe my luck. I'd been trying for months to get some kind of close contact with him once he returned to London, came back to Kara's house, without raising his suspicions. The French police were furious that he'd given them the slip. He was wanted there for crimes other than taking part in the student riots.'

'So how did that have anything to do with me? I wasn't living at Kara's then. When he came back I took everything at face value, thought it was no more than some kind of disagreement between him and Kara.'

Simon looked down at the carpet, avoiding my gaze. 'There's no easy way to say this. I was invited to Sylvia's party and you were there. What's more you were living in the very same house as Gabriel.'

'So, you, you used me...' I exploded.

'Oh, for goodness sake, Alison.'

Now he sounded cross.

'I may have been pleased to have found a way to make direct contact with Gabriel through you, but I would hardly have married you and kept on being married if I'd only wanted to find a way to Gabriel.'

Even I, in my fragile state, had to admit this was very unlikely.

'Anyway, it was all a long time ago and as you know the situation was resolved, or we thought it was resolved, by Gabriel's apparent death. We were sure we'd covered our tracks really well.'

He paused and looked at me anxiously.

'When you came home that day last November, I thought it was no more than some kind of aberration, some trick of your memory. I didn't want you to become involved with all that stuff from the past. I know how long it took you to recover from the accident.'

A bit of me still couldn't forgive him for the deception, wasn't going to let him get away with keeping this from me all these years. 'You must have had some idea.' I thought about the diary. 'What I don't understand is why you went to such lengths, hiding my diary, taking out those pages that would have helped me make sense of it all.'

He frowned, tapped his fingers on the arm of the chair, refusing to answer my question.

'Alison, you must remember that none of this matters any more. Now it appears anything is tolerated in this country and crimes committed by people like Gabriel seem very small beer indeed. It was a different time, a different world.'

'What do you mean "covered your tracks"...what is that all about?'

'All you have to know is that decisions were made, orders we carried out to make sure Gabriel's identity could never be discovered.'

'But George,' I whispered. 'He took over George's identity; he ruined Melanie's life...' I trailed off.

'It wasn't meant to be like that, Alison, but we needed names, proof of far bigger fish than Gabriel. He agreed to provide that information in return for saving his own skin, for all the charges being dropped.'

'Don't tell me you were involved in poor George's murder in order to save Gabriel?'

Pulling away my hands, I shrank further from his touch. It was bad enough to be almost certain that Gabriel had been a murderer, but surely not my own husband?

Simon shook his head again.

'No, that was nothing to do with us. There was no proof, but the word was that George saw Gabriel as a way of getting rich once he found out about the drug dealing. He didn't know about anything else, what was really happening, about the links to the subversive organisations. He underestimated Gabriel, completely.'

He waited for a moment, again appearing to be judging my reaction. With a sudden flash of insight I realised this had also been a problem for him, the difficulty of keeping this secret life of his from me all these years.

'But what about Kara? Did Gabriel have something to do with her death as well?'

Simon shrugged and said, 'It was a time of confusion. We were all trying to keep things under control. When Kara died, there wasn't any way we could accuse Gabriel, even if he was involved. By then he'd been granted immunity from prosecution. Because he spilled the beans the authorities were able to round up the ringleaders, stop what might have been truly disastrous consequences.' He gave a sigh. 'Or at least that's the way it seemed at the time.'

'How could you? How could you let him get away with killing Kara as well? What had she ever done?'

Simon looked down at his hands, cracked his knuckles, leaving a long pause before replying.

'She threatened to expose him. In the end she knew she was dying, it didn't matter what happened to her, but it was all a question of timing.'

My head felt as if it was about to explode as I sat there, trying to make sense of what Simon was saying. I'd wasted all these months, ruined my life by worries and in the end the problems weren't mine, were nothing to do with me.

Hurriedly Simon went on, 'There was no proof, no evidence. George may have been murdered or it may have been an accident. And Kara did die, but she was dying anyway. Whether Gabriel had anything to do with it…'

He shrugged, left the end of the sentence hanging in the air.

'Do you want me to become involved again after all this time? You shut me out, Alison. If you'd been more honest with me, we might have been able to tackle this together. I would have told you the whole story. But as it was…' he sighed, knowing there was no more to be said. It was all so long ago, in a different world, with different rules.

And he was right. I'd lied to him, had gone about chasing Gabriel's ghost in my own stubborn way. If I'd been honest, if I'd confided in him, I would have saved myself all the problems of the last few months.

Now I had to trust him: there was no other option. I might never know the whole truth, no one could after all these years, but I knew enough.

And whatever had happened, there was nothing wrong with my mind, there had been no relapse. It was all because my version of the past had been so wrong, so mistaken.

Simon was right. It had all happened at a time when very different rules applied.

He stood up and pulled me to my feet. 'Come on, Alison, it's all over. Let's get on with our lives.'

EPILOGUE

The ferry journey from Wemyss Bay to Rothesay on the north side of the isle of Bute is a short one, but that stretch of the Firth of Clyde separates two different worlds.

As soon as the boat left the port and headed out on to the water to a cacophony of screaming and swooping seagulls, my heart lifted and the sea breezes blew away all the cares of life in the city, the problems of the past few months.

Never had I needed the break more than now. Simon and I stood on the upper deck, close together but not speaking, each of us with our own thoughts. Of course I'd eventually had to tell Simon the whole story, what I'd been doing, or attempting to do. Not all at once, but a sketchy outline, filled in over a number of days. I was still too upset to shrug it off as he urged me.

Simon's explanation of events had helped, but finding out the truth about Gabriel had consumed too much of my life to allow me to dismiss it all in a casual way.

On reflection, not telling Simon in the beginning, when I'd first seen Gabriel on that train from Edinburgh, had been the right decision, because he would only have tried to stop me. That brief glimpse of Gabriel was no more than a bit of bad luck, and it was a relief to know there was nothing wrong with me, I was as well as I'd ever be.

So much had changed in the past few weeks, none of it as a direct result of this episode. Deborah had decided to go back to Art College and Susie had applied for an exchange post in America.

'It's what I need,' she'd said defiantly when I'd expressed astonishment. 'I've split up with Ross - a complete change of scene is the only answer. I don't want to be anywhere near him.'

'But such a long way?'

She refused to discuss it. 'My mind's made up, Alison. It will only be for a year.'

Perhaps it was as well we had booked this holiday in Bute, away from everything.

It was Simon who'd noticed in yesterday's paper, tucked away among the small items of home news, the story of an unidentified body washed up on the beach at Ayr. He pointed it out to me without saying a word but even before I read the description I guessed it had to be Gabriel. Perhaps this was what Gabriel had meant by moving on, or else something much more sinister. He'd become a problem for so many people.

In the end I didn't go to Melanie's funeral, though I considered it, but Josie left me a message to say it wouldn't be appropriate and I was in no mood to protest.

For a moment I'd thought about lifting the phone and informing the police that the body might be Gabriel's. Again I didn't. What was the point of raking all that up again? If they did get information, they would identify him as George King. I'd no proof of anything and it was better not to be involved.

They were all dead: Kara, George, Melanie and now Gabriel. There was no one left who might be harmed. And who was to care if his moving on was an accident or not?

With every mile the ferry cut through the water, the events of the past few months receded, took on an air of unreality, and the past was left further and further behind.

It could still be chilly out on the gusty waters of the Firth of Clyde even at this time of year and, shivering, I pulled my coat tightly around me.

'Are you all right, Alison?' Simon tightened his arms round me, a look of concern on his face.

Perhaps he was also feeling guilty; guilty for all those years when he had hidden from me the strange world he was entangled in, exactly what his role had been.

'I'm fine, really I am. It's just that, you know…' My voice tailed off, my words caught adrift and disappearing on the wind.

It seemed impossible to believe so much had happened in such a short time. In a way it had brought us closer, made us realise that secrets can come back to haunt you years later and that honesty is best, no matter how hurtful it might be.

'Would all passengers please return to their cars,' boomed the voice over the tannoy.

We headed down the narrow steps to the car deck as the ferry swung round into the calm waters of Rothesay Bay, ready to dock at the pier.

The cars rolled off one by one, past those cars waiting to board for the return trip. I glanced over, and for a moment thought it was Gabriel sitting in the car at the front of the line. But this time I knew for certain it was no more than my imagination at work.

I looked away, as I should have done all those months ago in Waverley station. The past is best left in the past, for we cannot change it.

We turned right and headed out of Rothesay along the shore road, past the Art Deco Pavilion, past the shady Skeoch woods, to take the road that leads to the village of Port Bannatyne on the far side of the town. The sun was shining, glinting on the waters of the Clyde, sparkling, dancing. I stole a glance at Simon as he concentrated on the road ahead.

Then I looked ahead also. Whatever it might bring, the future, not the past, was my concern now.

ACKNOWLEDGEMENTS

With thanks to everyone who kindly commented and made suggestions on the previous edition of this novel. Their time and patience is much appreciated.

Lightning Source UK Ltd.
Milton Keynes UK
UKOW01f0225010416

271298UK00001B/4/P